Peril in Palmanova

A Sanford 3rd Age Club Mystery (#15)

David W. Robinson

Discover us online:
www.crookedcatbooks.com

Join us on facebook:
www.facebook.com/crookedcatbooks

Tweet a photo of yourself holding
this book to **@crookedcatbooks**
and something nice will happen.

About the Author

A Yorkshireman by birth, David Robinson is a retired hypnotherapist and former adult education teacher, now living on the outskirts of Manchester with his wife and crazy Jack Russell called Joe (because he looks like a Joe).

A freelance writer for almost 30 years, he is extensively published, mainly on the web and in small press magazines. His first two novels were published in 2002 and are no longer available. His third novel, The Haunting at Melmerby Manor was published by Virtual Tales (USA) in 2007. He writes in a number of genres, including crime, sci-fi, horror and humour, and all his work has an element of mystery. His alter-ego, Flatcap, looks at the modern world from a cynical, 3rd age perspective, employing various levels of humour from subtle to sledgehammer.

A devout follower of Manchester United, when he is not writing, he enjoys photography, cryptic crosswords, and putting together slideshow trailers and podcast readings from his works.

David's online blog is at: **http://www.dwrob.com**

By the same author

Peril in Palmanova

A Sanford 3rd Age
Club Mystery (#15)

Chapter One

To Joe Murray's way of thinking, the Palmanova Corona was just about the oddest hotel he had ever stayed in.

Set amongst a clutch of hotels at the top of a rocky hill on the outskirts of Palmanova, an area known as Terrenova, the Corona was, to all intents and purposes, upside down. Passing through automatic, double glass doors from the street into the smart, angular lobby, the guests found themselves on floor five of seven. The two levels above consisted of suites, and the four floors below were apartments and studios. Add to that a convivial lounge bar, part of it in the open air beyond the lobby on floor 5, two swimming pools, an open sunbathing terrace and large showbar on the fourth, and it made for a convoluted and confusing arrangement.

But, as he frequently reminded himself, he had not come to Majorca with his friends from the Sanford 3rd Age Club to puzzle his way through an architectural anomaly. He was on holiday, taking a much-needed break from the virulent and debilitating stress of the last two months. And if nothing else, the easy way of life, persistent sunshine and the view from of Palmanova Bay from his balcony helped bring a sense of peace to a world full of pain.

From the open plateau of the sun terrace, with its two swimming pools, and its paved floor crowded with sun loungers upon which the seekers of the perfect tan passed the daylight hours, lay an uninterrupted view of Palmanova Bay, a vast, natural indentation on Majorca's south coast. Following the coastline on the far side of the bay, Joe could see all the way round to Palma, twenty kilometres away, further to the airport, and on to the resort of El Arenal, which he guessed was about fifty kilometres distant.

The calm waters immediately below the hotel were busy with private yachts, at least one of which, a gleaming white sixty-footer flying the flag of Spain, must have cost anything up to eighty million. Possibly more.

At times, other, local boats made their way out or back into the bay carrying what Joe assumed were tourists, and indeed one of them, named *Esmeralda,* boasted along its sides that it was a glass-bottomed. Jet skis could be seen zipping between the moored boats, and now and again he caught sight of a speedboat skipping along and drawing a water skier in its wake.

Away to the west, to Joe's left, a small beach was populated with more sun-worshippers, and behind it was the town, a higgledy-piggledy arrangement of buildings; shops, restaurants, interspersed with the high-rise blocks of modern hotels. Palmanova appealed to the wallets of the lower middle class/upper working class, modern British tourist, and Joe was proud of his status in the latter category.

He and the other members of the Sanford 3rd Age Club had arrived two days previously, and if he were brutally honest Joe would admit that getting off the plane at Palma Airport came as a great relief.

The death of Denise Latham had been a huge shock. The police would not have it, but as far as he was concerned, it was murder, not a road traffic accident. The car had been deliberately run off the road, and the other driver had not stopped. Worse, Denise was driving Joe's car and it was safe to assume that he was the target, not her.

Her death brought to an end a peaceful and stable period in Joe's life. He could not recall any time when he had been happier, more content, than in the two years he had lived with her, and with her passing he had sunk into a depression tinged with an extreme caution, forever looking over his shoulder for her killer coming back to take another shot at him.

Palmanova acted as a release valve for that pressure, but in the quieter moments such as now, while Sheila and

Brenda slept on loungers alongside of him, his thoughts drifted back to Denise and her violent end. She was younger than Joe; barely fifty years of age. It was not her time. She should be here with him now, not lying in a cold grave in a churchyard in South Leeds.

They had never talked about love. They were partners, they enjoyed life together, and naturally they shared a bed, and so it still should be. She should be here, alongside him, soaking up the ultraviolet, drinking down the vodkas with the tiniest dash of tonic, jiggling on the dance floor like a ridiculous born-again teenager, to music that Joe could barely comprehend.

It was all so sad, and the best he could hope for was that Palmanova would take away some of the pain.

Brenda stirred, reaching an arm down between the loungers, groped around until she found her wristwatch. Lifting it up, pushing her sunglasses up onto her forehead, she screwed up her eyes against the strong sunlight, and checked the time.

"It's almost noon," Joe told her. "Another hour before you need feeding."

She rolled onto her side facing him, and the top half of her bikini fell away. She chuckled. "Look the other way, Joe. I don't want you getting all hot and bothered."

Joe obliged and studied the sleek lines of the billionaire's yacht in the bay. "The way I feel just lately, you'd be hard-pressed to raise my interest beyond tepid."

Brenda adjusted her bikini, reaching behind to fasten it safely into place. "I'm peckish, and you know I like the occasional snack between meals. Besides, I'm thirsty." She sat up, swinging her tanned legs into the gap between her lounger and Joe's. Reaching for her purse she asked, "Soft drink or something a little stronger?"

"Booze? At this hour?"

Brenda laughed again. "A glass of beer in the middle of the day doesn't make you an alky. Now, what do you want?"

"I'll just have a cola." Joe turned his head in the other

direction, and raised his voice a little. "You want anything, Sheila, while Brenda is at the bar?"

Sheila's response was tired and sluggish, not much more than a grunt. "Lemonade."

With that, Brenda got to her feet and padded off towards the pool bar.

As she wandered away one of the entertainment staff came towards them. There were three or four of them, and they could be seen roaming about the place at different times of the day making an effort to energise the holidaymakers. They were all slender and athletically fit, young women, responsible for pool activities such as table tennis, darts and even archery during the day, while presenting some of the entertainment in the evenings.

They were easily recognised by their blue shorts and bright orange T-shirts with the word *ANIMACIÓN* written across the back of the shirt in large, dark blue letters. Joe's Spanish was limited but to him it translated as 'animation'. Regardless of the potential losses and gains in translation, he did not feel animated and had no desire to be.

The woman, Anna according to her nametag, was carrying a bow and an empty quiver. It was a daily ritual. She was seeking wannabe competitors for an archery contest, for which the winner would receive a gold medal (or gold-coloured plastic, medal) a certificate of excellence (handwritten in garish blue ink) and a bottle of Sangria (value €4.99) none of which, so it seemed to Joe, was worth the effort of getting to his feet let alone faffing about with an ancient weapon taking part in a sport he had never practised in his life.

In the two days since they arrived, Anna, or one of our colleagues, had approached him and other members of the 3rd Age Club trying to encourage their participation, but Joe had always declined with a wan smile and rueful shake of the head.

He did it again as Anna came towards him.

"Ah, Mister Joe, you disappoint me." Anna had a smile in her voice matched by the one on her lips and the sparkle in her green eyes. Her English was excellent but it was delivered with a strong, local accent. "You don't want to pull the strings on my bow?"

Joe chuckled. "Do you know what we mean by innuendo?" He did not wait for an answer for no other reason than he did not want to get into the debate. "I'm sorry, Anna, but I'm no Robin Hood."

The smile never left her lips and a small frown of puzzlement furrowed her brow. "Robin who?"

"He was a famous English Archer back in the middle ages and he used to... Never mind. It'd take too long to explain. Thank you, but I have no wish to demonstrate my lack of skills with a bow and arrow. I just want to lie here and steal some of your sunshine."

Anna giggled and gave him a friendly pat on the shoulder. "Enjoy your day."

Joe watched her shapely behind wander off seeking fresh targets.

Sheila raised her head, tracked his line of sight and tutted. "She's far too young for you, Joe."

"I'm working on memory, trying to remember what it was like when I was her age."

"Whatever it was like you were not using a bow and arrow to aim at the bullseye."

Joe grunted. It could have signalled humour or disapproval. "More innuendo."

He lay back on the lounger, pulled the peak of his baseball cap down so the shadow shielded his Ray Bans and eyes from the powerful sunlight. The brief exchange had taken away thoughts of Denise, but as Sheila had drifted off to sleep once again, and he allowed his mind to wander, the memories and pain returned.

His powers of observation and skill as a private detective had made him his fair share of enemies down the years. Any number of people had been sent to prison as a result of his doggedness. Many of them were murderers, and he did not know just how many were out on licence. It was reasonable to assume that there would be people out there seeking to wreak vengeance upon him.

Denise, too, was a private investigator, but she worked almost exclusively for insurance companies. Prior to that she had been a Detective Sergeant with the West Yorkshire police, and once again it was safe to say that there were people out there, on the street, bearing grudges against her.

Who, then, was the target of that hit and run?

There was no way of knowing, and even his niece, Detective Inspector Gemma Craddock, of Sanford CID refused to accept that it was anything more than a road traffic accident and the perpetrator had cleared off rather than face the consequences of his/her actions.

Joe was one of those people blessed with great self-knowledge. There was little anyone could tell him about himself that he did not already know but in this case he had to wonder if his suspicions were simply an attempt to rationalise Denise's demise; a theory born of his investigative abilities to help him make sense of her death. At those times when his thinking was clearest, he would agree with Gemma. There was absolutely nothing to corroborate the notion that the car had been deliberately run off the road, and it was, indeed, the result of a moment's dangerous inattention on the part of the other driver.

Accident or not, the driver should be brought to book. Analysis of paint scrapes deposited on Joe's wrecked car told police that they were looking for a pale blue Fiat Punto, which was at least five years old. There was no CCTV anywhere in the vicinity of the collision, and there were thousands of such cars on the road. Without further evidence, without eye-witnesses, it was a futile task, and Gemma, acting as his main liaison, freely admitted that the driver was unlikely to be traced and prosecuted. It was a frustrating state of affairs, but it was as it was and there was nothing anyone could do about it.

Sheila and Brenda, both long-standing widows, had been supportive. As well as working for him, they had been two of his closest friends since the schoolyard half a century ago, and they knew him better than his own mother and father had. Their experience of widowhood, after long and happy marriages, meant they understood Joe's angst, and they sympathised, encouraged him to talk, urged him to get it all out of his system so that the grief could follow its natural course. Somewhere, in the not too distant future, life would return to normal. Denise would never be forgotten. She would be a permanent gap in that adjusted life, but the memories which brought him such pain right now would recur with greater fondness.

Brenda returned from the bar, snapping him out of his depressed reverie. She distributed drinks – lemonade for Sheila, cola for Joe and a light beer for herself – and perched on her lounger, sipping gratefully from her glass.

Sheila sat up and swallowed a mouthful of lemonade. Speaking across Joe, addressing Brenda, she said, "His lordship has been eyeing up the young women, again."

A broad, lascivious grin spread across Brenda's face. "I like ambition in a man, and let's face it, if Joe fancies his chances with Anna, that is seriously ambitious."

Joe savoured the bite of carbonated soft drink sliding down his throat, temporarily quenching his thirst. It gave him a few brief seconds to think up a riposte to Brenda's jibe. "There's many a good tune played on an old fiddle, and I'm still quite a catch, you know."

And Brenda patted him on the knee. "Anna is only after your money, Joe."

"Well, she's wasting her time, isn't she? I keep telling you, I'm a poor man, destined for a life of poverty on the pension."

Sheila tittered. "That's just your excuse; the one you roll out when we want a pay rise."

"Pampered. That's what you are, you two. If you'd work for my dad, you'd have known about slavery. Do you know, when I was thirteen years old, he was dragging me out of bed at half past four every morning to go to the wholesale markets with him and pick up the fresh fruit and veg for the café."

"Here we go again, wandering down memory lane."

9

Brenda put down her glass and made to play an imaginary violin. "Now it's me playing a good tune with an old fiddle."

"With friends like you two, I don't need enemies threatening to snuff me out."

The come in was intended as a risible response to Brenda's last gag, but it backfired and the general mood fell flat.

Sheila put it into words. "Please don't start that again, Joe."

"Sorry. I didn't mean to. But it keeps coming back to me. I can't get over thinking—"

Brenda cut him off. "The moment you have any evidence, then you can take it forward, but for now you have to force yourself to bury it. We're here to help, Joe, but you have to help yourself."

"Yeah, yeah, I get the message." He downed another mouthful of cola, and stood up. "I'll take a walk around. See if I can shake myself out of this pit of misery."

Determined not to give them the opportunity to respond, he sauntered off towards the safety rail at the edge of the sun terrace.

Weaving his way through the crowded area he passed Les Tanner and his lady friend, Sylvia Goodson, sheltering in the shade of an open sun umbrella. Sylvia was asleep while Les was sat upright reading an old Alistair MacLean novel. As Joe passed, Les gave him a curt nod of acknowledgement, which Joe barely returned. Although there was no real animosity between them, the two men had never been the best of friends. Les believed Joe to be administratively inefficient, especially in regard to the running of the 3rd Age Club, and by turn Joe considered Les to be a nit-picking pedant who, having once held the rank of captain in the Territorial Army, lived in the past, enraptured by tales of wars he had never fought.

Moving further on, he passed Alec and Julia Staines, enjoying the sun on their near-naked bodies, and from Joe's point of view, for all their advancing years, they still looked good. Alec was still a slim, trim and muscular man, and Julia had a shapely figure which she was not afraid to show off under the tiniest of bikinis.

Alongside them, George Robson and his best buddy, Owen Frickley, both employed in manual capacities by Sanford Borough Council, were sleeping off the previous night's drink. Just old enough to be members of the 3rd Age Club, where the minimum age was fifty, both were divorced, just like Joe, but he envied them their freewheeling lifestyle, a constant cycle of work, drink, women, work, drink, women... Or so they claimed. In addition, they were tough nuts, more than capable of handling themselves in the event of trouble. No sane, potential murderer would go anywhere near them. Joe was a much easier target.

He reached the safety rail, composed of a line of waist-high, toughened glass panes, and leaned upon it looking out across the bay.

Esmeralda was making her way to the tiny quay in the near corner off Palmanova Bay, bringing back another load of sightseers who had probably enjoyed the subsurface vision of the sea life in the shallow waters. A paraglider floated by, nestling comfortably in his harness a hundred feet above speedboat towing him, and as both he and Joe looked around the bay, the engines of one or two boats could be seen to churn the water. With the sun approaching its zenith, the beach appeared more crowded than ever, and the pace of life in this idyllic little town slowed to a crawl. It was simply a perfect day.

A sibilant thud attracting Joe's attention, and he turned his head in the direction of the sound.

Five yards to his right, the archery competition was under way. A gaggle of men and women surrounded Anna as she demonstrated her skills with the weapon. A tall, wooden screen, painted white to match the rest of the building, had been erected to facilitate the archery. Any arrow missing the target would clink into the wall and drop safely to the floor, rather than shooting over the rail and out into the bay. And, of course, the immediate vicinity was kept clear of sun loungers.

It held no interest for Joe, and he returned to staring out across the bay.

Movement from below caught his attention. Looking over the rail, it was a sheer drop of about fifty feet to a wooded bank, inaccessible from land. In the crystal clear, green waters of the shallows, a young couple negotiated a dinghy, and peered down into the water as they paddled slowly along.

For a moment, Joe wondered what it was they had seen…or thought they had seen. From up here, he could see the bottom, but it was no more than an undulating, impossible jigsaw puzzle, and the only thing moving were the ripples on the surface.

There was a loud buzz in his right ear. For a brief moment, Joe thought it was some large insect coming too close to him. He raised his hand to brush it away, but before he could, a flash of white, tailed with multi-coloured fins flashed past his ear and out across the waters, where its trajectory brought it arcing down into the sea.

Joe whirled and stared at a horrified Anna as she hurried towards him. But the bow was on the ground where she and other competitors were shooting from.

Chapter Two

Anna rushed across to the safety rail. Her eyes were stark, her tanned features pale, and when she spoke it was in a trembling voice close to breaking. "Mister Joe. Are you all right? I am so sorry. It was an accident."

Joe was trembling, too. He looked sideways to the target area and mentally estimated the distance at about five yards. "An accident? Not from where I'm standing. Who the hell fired that arrow?"

The first hint of tears sparkled in Anna's eyes. "It was Ms Killington. She is new in, yesterday. She was aiming for the target, but at the last moment, she staggered and her aim went wide. I told her to be careful. I am sorry, Mister Joe."

His mind frantic with numerous notions, many of them bordering on paranoia, Joe made an effort to soothe her worries. "It's not your fault, Anna, but you're likely to get blamed. Where is this Ms Killington?"

She waved in the vague direction of the firing line where her competitors were still grouped. "She is over… Oh. She has gone."

Joe's racing thoughts zoomed in, their focus narrowing to only one possibility. "Get onto your boss. I want the police called."

Anna's pretty face underwent another transformation, her eyes widening, mouth falling open. "The police?"

"This was no accident. It was an attempt on my life."

***

Chief Superintendent Donald Oughton had been station commander for more years than Gemma Craddock cared to remember. He was a popular chief; one who let his teams get on with their job with the minimum of interference, but he was also a stickler for the rule book and he demanded they keep him informed of developments or non-developments as the case may be.

In his mid to late fifties, he had made it by the traditional route, starting as a beat bobby in the mid-seventies, and along the way he had done his stints in almost all departments. A tall, slender and a lugubrious man, he was also a friend of Joe Murray. Gemma had the notion they had been at school together.

And she believed it was that friendship which caused Oughton the greater worry when she sat with him just after three in the afternoon.

"You spoke to your uncle?" Oughton asked.

Gemma nodded and hastily buried a flash of irritation. She was a Detective Inspector and yet everyone, whether to her face or behind her back, still referred to her as Joe Murray's niece.

The telephone conversation with Joe had been difficult. Aside from the one-thousand-mile distance, his mobile kept losing its signal, and he was in an excitable mood, so it was not always easy to understand what he was saying.

"I thought he was on away on holiday."

"He's in Majorca, sir."

"What? And he's still on about Denise Latham's death?"

Gemma felt compelled to defend her uncle. "To be fair, he was with living with her, and they'd been in a relationship since the Kilburn-Corbin business, two years back. But, that's not why he rang, sir. He says someone has tried to kill him at the hotel where he's staying. Shot at him with a bow and arrow, apparently."

Oughton clucked. "He originally said that the crash which killed Denise was meant for him. We never turned up any evidence of that, did we?" He drummed agitated fingers on the desk. "Tell me something honestly, Gemma. Is Joe losing the plot?"

She sighed. "I really don't know, sir." Even as she said

the words a lance of pain shot through her. It felt as if she were betraying her favourite uncle, a man who had gone out of his way to encourage her when she first joined the police service. True, Joe had been a pain in the backside many times during her fifteen-year career, but more often than not he had been proved right. He rarely got it wrong, but this time… "I spoke to a local police officer, an Inspector Gallego, and he confirmed that there had been some kind of an incident at the hotel involving archery equipment, but he's still investigating, and according to the entertainment staff at the place it was an accident. Joe was lucky to escape without injury. That much is true. But that doesn't make it an attempt on his life."

Oughton remained silent for a moment, taking in the information. "Let's go out on a limb, and say that there really is a plot to kill Joe. Anyone in the frame?"

Gemma shrugged. "There are plenty of people who might have a downer on him, but most of them are still inside and it's easy enough to check on those who might be out on licence." Again she hesitated briefly before pressing on. "With the best will in the world, sir, I think Joe might just be stressed out. I think he's still grieving for Denise. But if you want me to follow it up, I will do."

Oughton shifted in his seat, abandoning his relaxed pose, swivelling the chair round to face her, becoming more businesslike. "Do that, Gemma, and keep me informed."

***

An hour earlier, and a thousand miles away, a host of people, amongst them, Brenda, Sheila, and Anna, struggled to calm an agitated Joe in the face of his insistence that the arrow was a deliberate attempt to kill or injure him.

As any of these friends would testify, once Joe's mind was made up, it was extraordinarily difficult to persuade him that he might be wrong. It was even harder in this instance because by the time Anna had ascertained that he was uninjured, the woman who had fired the rogue arrow

15

had completely disappeared, and no one, not even amongst the archery competitors, had noticed where she went.

Inspector Gallego and a junior officer from the *Policia Nacional* arrived twenty minutes later, and listened to the various accounts of what had happened. Gallego, a tall and muscular, square-shouldered man, maintained an air of polite interest in the face of Joe's increasing anger, and promised to investigate.

By the time he had completed his basic enquiries, and returned to the pool, Joe was on the telephone talking to Gemma, and eventually, he handed over the phone for the Spanish police officer to talk to his opposite number in Sanford.

While this was taking place, Sheila made another effort to calm Joe down. "You're overreacting, Joe. It was an accident."

"So how come the woman's done a runner?"

"She's probably half drunk, Joe," Brenda suggested, "and the accident scared the hell out of her. In her shoes I'd have probably run for it."

Joe fumed. "Why do I get the impression that no one is listening to me? This Killington woman was five or six yards off target. That was not an accident."

A few yards from them, Gallego bid Gemma 'adios' then returned Joe's phone. "Señor Murray, having spoken to your niece, Señorita Craddock, I learned that you have recently lost your partner in a tragic accident. It is understandable that you imagine this arrow was fired at you deliberately, but there is nothing to suggest that this is the case. Ms Killington has gone out, left the hotel, but I will need to speak to her, and I will do so the moment she returns. For now, I recommend that you relax, enjoy a drink, the sunshine, and our Spanish hospitality, and please, try to keep yourself calm."

"Leaving her free to have another go at me? Not bloody likely." Joe stormed away leaving Sheila and Brenda to reassure the inspector that they would look after him.

Back on his sun lounger, Joe seethed with furious

impotence. None of them were prepared to take him seriously, and even his best friends were refusing to listen to him. He was a long way from home, but in the company of people he had known for years, and for all the good it would do him, he might just as well be alone in a hostile war zone.

* * *

Shown into the manager's office, Anna felt nervous as she sat opposite Inspector Gallego.

The policeman made no effort to ease her anxiety. "You are Anna Squillano, and you have worked here for one year. This is correct?"

She nodded. "Yes, sir."

"And you were in charge of the archery competition? This is so?"

Anna confirmed it once again.

"Tell me then, how did this Ms Killington come to take part in the competition?"

Anna, whose thoughts had been obsessed with the near miss ever since it happened, struggled to recall her efforts to recruit competitors.

"I cannot properly remember. She was, I think, sunbathing. I go round the pool when I am looking for people to take part, and I'm sure she was enjoying the sunshine and I asked her."

Gallego made a few notes. "You know this Ms Killington?"

"No, sir. I mean, I will have seen her around the hotel, the pool, the bar, but I cannot say that I have particularly noticed her."

Gallego scribbled on his pad again. "You have not noticed her, Miss Squillano, because she is not a guest that this hotel."

The declaration hit her like an electric shock. She began to tremble, her mind unable to accept the inspector's words. Across the desk, he waited patiently for her to reply, and she did not know what she was supposed to say.

17

"That is impossible, sir. She was wearing the silver wristband of the all-inclusive guest. How could she have that, if she was not staying here?"

"A good question, Miss Squillano. We have identified the woman on the hotel's security cameras. The image is poor, but as you say, she is wearing the wristband. It seems to me, that the only way she could have got one is if a member of staff gave it to her, and since you were the one who recruited her for this competition…" Gallego trailed off, leaving the implication hanging in the air.

Opposite him, Anna was near to tears. "It is nothing to do with me, sir. You must believe me. I know nothing of any of this. I am a sports and entertainments hostess. It is my job to help the guests enjoy their stay. Why would I help a complete stranger get access to the hotel facilities?"

"Perhaps you were paid to arrange it. You enjoy the bars in Palmanova during your time off, don't you?"

"Of course, but—"

Gallego cut her off. "Perhaps then, you met Ms Killington in a bar and she offered you money in exchange for the wristband."

"No, sir. This did not happen. I have never seen Ms Killington before today and possibly yesterday."

Gallego toyed with his pen. "I am not sure I believe you, Ms Squillano. I checked on your past history. You have a conviction for theft. So you are not afraid to break the law."

Tears flowed from Anna's eyes. "But that was years ago. I was a child. A schoolgirl. I had never done anything wrong, since. You cannot hold that against me now."

"I am investigating what appears to be an accident, and yet I have to consider the testimony of this Joe Murray that it may have been an attempt on his life. I do not say that this is so, but if it is, then it is clear that Ms Killington gained access to this hotel in order to carry out her attack on him. And to get into the hotel, she needed help. You, Ms Squillano, are the only employee who I can find who has been in trouble with the police. You may go for the moment, but I may need to speak to you again."

***

Shaded beneath overhead blinds, there was an area of tables close to the pool bar, where Brenda and Sheila sat together, taking a little respite from the searing temperatures of the hottest part of the day.

There was only one topic for discussion.

"I remember when he and Alison divorced," Brenda said, "and he wasn't this bad. I didn't realise he was so... I dunno... captivated by Denise."

"We're too close to him, dear. We work with him every day, and he's one of our best friends. We see every side of him but this. We see the grumpy, the snaps and snarls, we see the laughter when he gets round to enjoying himself, but we never see the love, the heartache or heartbreak because he buries it in his work." Sheila shook her head sadly. "The Lazy Luncheonette has a lot to answer for."

Brenda sniggered. "Don't let Joe hear you say that. The place is his life."

She concentrated on her glass of cola, running her hands gently along the sides, fascinated by the way her fingertips cleared the condensation.

"What is it, Brenda?"

Brenda looked up. "Hmm?"

"How long have we known each other? Fifty years? You have something on your mind. What is it?"

"Nothing. I just... well, I just wondered, you don't suppose he could be right, do you?"

Sheila drank from her own glass. "You mean is someone really trying to kill him? I think it's not beyond the bounds of possibility. He has enough enemies out there. But there is nothing to back it up. The accident which killed Denise really was an accident. A hit and run, for sure, but still an accident. And if this Killington woman really did aim for him today, then she's very silly. If you're going to follow Joe to Majorca just to bump him off, you don't do it on a crowded sun terrace in a busy hotel, do you?"

"Hmm, no. I suppose not." A new sense of urgency

came to Brenda. "But how do we get Joe to see this?"

"A good question." Looking beyond Joe's sleeping figure, Sheila spotted Anna making her rounds, this time seeking participants for a table tennis competition. "If we could get a word with Ms Killington, reassure her that Joe is not angry, that she's in no trouble, and get the pair of them face to face, would that help, do you think?"

Brenda's face expressed her doubts. "Not if Joe loses it."

"But we'd be there to make sure he doesn't."

As Anna drew near, Sheila signalled to her to join them.

The young woman smiled broadly. "You want to play ping-pong?"

Brenda laughed aloud and Sheila giggled. "No, dear. The mastery of inactivity is our ambition, and even table tennis is too involved for our ageing bodies."

Brenda chuckled again. "You speak for yourself, Sheila Riley. I keep my body active enough." She winked at Anna. "But not by playing table tennis."

Sheila moved to quell any confusion Brenda's innuendo might cause for Anna. "Actually, we were wondering whether you could persuade Ms Killington to join us, so we can get her and Joe talking face to face, and try to convince him that it was an accident."

Anna's face darkened and her smile faded. "I'm sorry, I cannot do that."

Her refusal took them both by surprise.

"We're not looking for trouble, Anna," Brenda said. "It's just that—"

"It is complicated," Anna interrupted. "Inspector Gallego tells me Ms Killington is not staying at the hotel. She should not have been here. She should not have been part of the competition." The tears formed in her eyes again. "And the police think I helped her get in."

Her crying elicited a wave of sympathy from the two women. Burying thoughts of the implications behind the news, Sheila took Anna's hand. "I'm sure he thinks nothing of the kind. Don't upset yourself, dear. You're a very pleasant, cheerful young lady and the inspector is probably just trying to unsettle you. Go about your work, Anna. We won't trouble you again."

Taking the encouraging smiles of both women with her, Anna went on her way, and their faces became grim.

Brenda put their feelings into words. "What the hell will Joe make of this when he finds out?"

"We know what he'll make of it, Brenda. We'll just have to be at our best to make sure he doesn't go over the edge."

Chapter Three

The centre of Palmanova was, to Joe's way of thinking, like so many other popular Spanish holiday resorts. Its streets were lined with the usual souvenir shops, tobacconists (the only shops where cigarettes could legally be bought over the counter) places selling slightly more upmarket clothing and shoes, and the inevitable bars and restaurants.

The place was biased towards the English, evident in a selection of bars with names readily recognisable to the Brits: The Prince William, Eastenders, The Cock & Bull, The Cutty Sark.

The morning after the archery incident, Joe, Sheila and Brenda ambled along towards the main square. He frowned on a group of bare-chested men sat outside an English bar, all of them rowdy and raucous and obviously worse for wear for drink.

Joe checked his watch. "Ten in the morning and they're drunk already."

"They probably never sobered up from last night," Brenda said. "Live and let live, Joe. They're not bothering us."

He frowned. "Palmanova is supposed to be slightly more upmarket than Magaluf, but you wouldn't think so looking at them."

"I've seen it all before," Sheila assured them. "In Benidorm and Playa de Las Américas. It was part of the reason Peter and I started visiting less touristy places."

The mention of her late husband, a police inspector in Sanford who had succumbed to two heart attacks following quickly one after the other, only served to remind Joe of Denise's demise, and his spirits sank once again.

Sheila, like Brenda, had been widowed for over a decade. Joe had to ask himself how had they coped with the gnawing emptiness left by the passing of their husbands.

He recalled the sadness at the deaths of his mother and father. Unmarried at the time of both deaths, The Lazy Luncheonette had demanded all his attention. He had little time for grieving.

Although not in the same class, the breakdown of his marriage was similarly traumatic, but once again the needs of the business superseded the need to deal with his own feelings.

As they wandered along the sunny streets, the women pausing occasionally to study window displays or browse around a cluttered souvenir shop, it occurred to Joe that he had no life; he had never had any life. The business, that demanding little cafeteria on Sanford's Doncaster Road had taken his life, and in return it had given him nothing more than financial security. It was, he reflected, a poor return. What use was money when it was all there was?

The anger began to build in him again, and he had to make a conscious effort to suppress it. For two years, Denise had shown him how to enjoy himself, and that it did not depend on money. She had been taken, and for the first time in his life he was dealing with genuine grief.

In an effort to sidestep his turgid feelings, he considered Sheila and Brenda. He had known these women for fifty years, and in that time they had, all three of them, suffered the usual ups and downs, joys and sadness, laughter and tears, but unlike the women, Joe had brushed aside the emotional rollercoaster, dismissed it as inconsequential. Was it any wonder he was so irritable much of the time?

Thoughts of the two women reminded him of the previous evening in the hotel bar. A pianist played easy-listening tunes, providing a melodic background to the hum of conversation. As the sun set on Palmanova Joe questioned them on the mysterious Ms Killington, only for Sheila to look around and say the woman was not there.

"I saw you talking to Anna after lunch. Didn't she have

anything to say?"

Brenda answered. "It's against hotel policy for the staff to get involved in this kind of thing. She apologised, naturally, but she refused point blank to point out the Killington woman."

The answer had come too quickly for Joe's liking. It smacked of a rehearsed response, which, by default, meant it was untrue. Throughout the evening as the dusk turned to night, the brighter stars came out, and the lights of Palmanova glimmered along the curved coastline of the bay in a pleasant show of seaside illuminations, Joe occasionally pushed his friends gently on the matter, but elicited no further information.

They were obviously hiding something, and he knew them well enough to know that they were doing so in deference to his fragile state of mind. They had not realised that softly-softly, kid gloves were not what he needed. He wanted straight talking, but breakfast at the hotel had produced no change in their approach. They played the innocents and refused to tell him what it was they knew.

Strolling into the centre of Palmanova, Sheila and Brenda stepped into what looked like a mid-range clothing shop. Joe stood outside, basking in the warm sun, and looked around seeking something, anything, to occupy his mind. Across the street was another parade of shops; a bank, shoe shop, a couple of bars and cafés, and in the centre of the row, the large, brown logo of an officially licensed tobacconist.

Lifting his shirt, he fished into his money belt, pushed his wallet and passport to one side and came out with a €20 note. Joe was notoriously fickle. All holiday hotels provided room safes (for hire, usually at about €10 a week) but Joe did not trust them. For all he knew, the cleaning staff could have copies of the key. For that reason he kept his passport, currency and wallet with him at all times.

Careful to remind himself that he needed to look left not right before stepping off the kerb, he crossed the road, went into the cigarette shop and came out a few minutes later with two packs of twenty and a couple of disposable lighters.

He crossed the road again, to an open square, where he could sit. He removed the cellophane wrapping from one pack, took out a cigarette and lit it. Drawing the smoke deep into his lungs, he suffered a violent coughing fit. His head spun and he squeezed his eyes tight shut to overcome the dizziness. He took another drag. The cough was less ferocious this time, and the wooziness less noticeable. He would get used to it.

"Joe, what are you doing?"

He opened his eyes to find Sheila and Brenda standing before him. Both appeared shocked.

"You haven't smoked for years," Sheila reminded him.

He defied her disapproval. "Yes, and I'm busy recalling just what I've been missing."

They sat either side of him, and Brenda took his hand. "We know how stressed you are, Joe, but while the tobacco might give you a high, it won't take the stress away."

"But it will aggravate your COPD," Sheila said.

In a show of determined resistance, Joe took another drag on a cigarette and blew out the smoke with a long, satisfied hiss.

"Just a few weeks ago, some nutter killed my girlfriend. Yesterday, another nutter tried to kill me. You two know more than you're telling me, and none of you, not you, the other third-agers, not the police back home or in this country believe me. And you expect me to worry about the damage a cigarette is going to do to my lungs? Well, get this: I – don't – care." He punctuated the words with short pauses. "Not anymore. Let the stupid tart snuff me out. I'm going to enjoy myself." He took another drag, crushed out the cigarette and promptly lit another. "Now, did I see a lap-dancing club somewhere in this town?"

His final words had the necessary effect. The two women were white-faced with shock.

"Joe—"

He cut Sheila off. "Tell me what it is you know. Tell me

25

what you found out that you think I need protecting from."

There was a lengthy silence filled only by the background sounds of a seaside town coming to life as holidaymakers stepped out into the sunshine.

They could hardly have been surprised by Joe's candour. He had been abrupt, tell-it-as-it-is all his life, sometimes to the point of rudeness, and they were perfectly used to it. He interpreted their silence, therefore, as an unspoken, internalised debate on what to say and how to say it, and each was waiting for the other to speak first.

Eventually it was Sheila who began, relating the tale Anna had told them the previous afternoon. Brenda put in occasional comments, and they shared their reasoning behind the refusal to tell Joe what they had learned.

"We were thinking of you," Brenda pleaded in an effort to exculpate themselves from his accusing stare.

"We did what we did with the best of intentions," Sheila assured him.

"The road to hell." Joe took another drag on his second cigarette and crushed it out on the stubber attached to a nearby litter bin. "Translating all this, what you mean is, you thought telling me that I was right would send me over the top. How would you have felt if this bloody lunatic had come for me last night and left me dead? Did it not occur to you that if you'd told me I would, at least, have been on my guard?"

Brenda patted his hand. "You've been very stressed out —"

Joe snatched his hand back, and cut her off. "For god's sake, stop treating me like a child. Yes, I'm hurting over what happened to Denise. I miss her. But I'm in no flaming hurry to join her. I am not gonna sit around Palmanova as an easy target for some nutter." He took a deep breath in an effort to calm down. "Do we know what progress the police have made?"

"No, we don't, and Inspector Garcia is not based in Palmanova."

Joe stood up. "In that case, it's up to the hotel to get the information for us. Come on."

Having been on the back foot for the last few minutes, Brenda and Sheila found their legendary resistance.

"Not so fast, buster."

Sheila was less Bogart/Cagney. "We have more shopping to do."

"You sit here and enjoy your little sticks of poison."

Joe took out a third cigarette and lit it. "Good enough. You know where to find me."

***

Back home, Gemma sat with the senior investigations manager of the North Shires Insurance Company, at their head office in Leeds.

Eliot Banks was aged about forty. A tall, bulky man with a slightly rough edge to his voice. The fingers of his large hands were decked with various gold rings, and behind the open collar of his white shirt and the loosely hanging, red, company tie, a thick, gold chain dangled around his neck. It was all designed to intimidate; to give the impression of a late-model, tough street cop, even though inquiries would revealed that Banks had never been a policeman.

The company was housed in a glass shoebox on Park Row, in the heart of the city's financial district, but Banks's office was at the rear of the building, overlooking a dingy yard, rather than the impressive, sunlit front of the block.

From the moment she joined him, Banks made an effort to impose his will upon the interview.

"We don't talk about investigations, Inspector. Whatever Denise Latham was working on, it's confidential and short of you coming back with a court order, I won't tell you anything."

Gemma greeted the confident announcement with a smile of calm equanimity. "And do you think, Mr Banks, that I wouldn't go for a court order? I'm simply trying to short-circuit that process and for a very good reason. You know what happened to Denise?"

27

"She was killed in a car crash."

"To be precise, her car was run off the road, and we have evidence to suggest that it was not an accident. In plain English, Mr Banks, words that even you can understand, we suspect that Denise may have been murdered. Now, with regard to insisting upon a court order, I can view that in several ways, one of which is an effort to obstruct our investigation. I would have to consider what motive you have for doing so, and the logical conclusion would be that you were involved in her murder." Gemma leaned forward to impress her grip upon the interview. "Am I making myself clear?"

Banks made the effort to wrest control back. "That's ridiculous. Even if you're right about her death, there's no way I'd be involved in anything like that."

"Then why do I need a court order?"

"Company policy."

"Stick your company policy where the sun doesn't shine. Denise was possibly murdered. Right now, there's been another attempt, this time aimed at her partner, Joe Murray. I don't know who's behind it, and I need to know what Denise was working on, and whether Joe was helping her, and you are standing in my way. It would help if you stopped pratting about and told me what I want to know."

"Look—"

"No, you look," Gemma interrupted. "Joe Murray also happens to be my uncle, and if anything happens to him because you're holding back, I will personally go through this company's past investigations until I find enough to crucify you. Now what was Denise working on when she was killed?"

Banks capitulated. He flounced out of his chair, yanked open the middle drawer of a filing cabinet, searched through for a few moments and withdrew a thick buff folder. Slamming the drawer shut, he returned to his seat, placed the folder on the blotter, opened it and spent a few moments reading through the top sheets.

At length, he looked up and at Gemma. "There's this

bloke in Harrogate. Builder. Fell off a ladder on a site, and reckons he can hardly walk. Health and Safety have already hammered the main contractor with a hefty fine, but he reckons he can never work again, and he's trying to stuff them for a coupla million. The contractor has, naturally, passed the claimed to us. We're their insurers. We asked Denise to look into it. We don't just poppy up two million dabs like that." He snapped his fingers to emphasise his meaning. "As far as we're aware, Denise had the bloke under surveillance, and trust me, she was good at that. Chances are, he didn't even know he was being watched."

Gemma chewed her lip. "She told Joe that her car had to come off the road for a day or two, which is why she borrowed his. I just wonder…" She snapped out of her reverie. "Is this builder known to the police?"

Banks shrugged. "You tell me. You people don't go out of your way to help us."

Gemma took out her notebook. "Give me his name and address. I'll go see him."

"I don't know…" Banks trailed off under her determined eye. He read the report again. "Thomas Higginshaw. Twenty-three, Tankersley Lane, Harrogate."

Gemma scribbled down the details, put away her pocketbook, and stood up. "Thank you, Mr Banks. I'll be in touch if I need any more information."

Chapter Four

By the time they had made their way up the steep hill to the Palmanova Corona, Joe, Sheila and Brenda were exhausted.

"I told you we should have taken a taxi," Brenda complained. "I'm sure it wouldn't have cost more than five euros."

Joe sat on a low wall outside the hotel entrance, dug into his pockets seeking his inhaler, found it and took two puffs. "Five… five euros is… is two pints in this place. Get your… priorities right."

Sheila looked down her nose at him. "You can hardly breathe thanks to that hill. Walk up and down it too often and you won't be here to enjoy those two pints."

Brenda kept up the pressure. Holding up three carrier bags full of clothing, she said, "Five euros is nothing to what I've spent this morning."

Joe fished into his pockets again, this time coming out with cigarettes and lighter, prompting another protest from Sheila.

"I don't believe you, Joe. Thirty seconds ago, you needed Ventolin to ease your breathing difficulties, and now you're about to take in more poison."

He lit the cigarette with an air of defiance, drew in the smoke, went through the usual coughing fit, and when he had control over his breathing again, he declared, "I'll stop again, when this banana has been caught and locked up. Or, at least, when you lot start taking me seriously."

"We are taking you seriously, Joe." Brenda took out a handkerchief and wiped the sweat from her brow. "We've admitted that it looks suspicious, but we still don't know anything for sure, and it's not an excuse for you to compromise your health with those things." She pointed at the cigarette.

Joe took another drag. "You might not be convinced, but I'm sure of it. If she gets the chance, I could be dead before the week is out, so why shouldn't I enjoy myself?"

The women knew that Joe in this kind of mood was not to be argued with, and silence fell as they sat in the sunshine.

Cars lined either side of the steep and narrow street. Mid-morning and there were people about: holidaymakers, easily identified by their skimpy attire of shorts and T-shirts, on their way down to the town or the beach, and others, obviously dressed for work, their shirts, long and short-sleeved, bearing the logos of hotels and other businesses, clearly labelling them as locals.

A large van trundled slowly down the hill, the driver negotiating his way slowly between the parked vehicles, taking care not to clip a bumper or wing mirror. As it passed them, a middle-aged woman on the other side of the street, heavily dressed in a long, flouncy skirt and dark top, dropped her shopping bag, spilling its contents across the pavement.

Joe tutted, put out his cigarette and hurried across the street to help her pick up the bread, fruit and other items.

"Gracias."

"De nada," Joe replied, demonstrating his limited Spanish.

As he turned to cross the street again, a car pulled out of its parking space forty yards further up the hill. Joe had already stepped into the road, and he was not worried. Spanish drivers, he knew, were far more tolerant than their British counterparts.

He was wrong.

With a roar, the car accelerated and came straight at him.

The woman he had helped shouted an unintelligible warning. Brenda screamed, "JOE!" Sheila could only stare in rigid mortification.

At the last possible second, with the car just yards away

and bearing down upon him, Joe threw himself back to the pavement he had just left. He felt the rush of the car's slipstream whistle past his foot, and the next thing he knew he was hitting the pavement, rolling over and his shoulder ramming into the property wall lining that side of the road.

The car tore off down the hill clipping another vehicle on the right and yet another on the left before disappearing at high speed towards the town.

The woman he had helped stood over him babbling in Spanish, none of which Joe understood. Getting groggily to his feet, he reassured her with gestures and by the time Sheila and Brenda had reached him both the woman and Joe had calmed down.

Brenda, speaking in broken, pidgin Spanish, further reassured the woman while Sheila concentrated on Joe.

"Are you all right?"

"Shaken and stirred but I'll live to fight another mission." He pinned her with a determined gleam in his eye. "Now do you believe me?"

Sheila, too, was shaking. "Yes. It doesn't make any sense, but it does look as if you're right."

Finished with the woman, Brenda joined the conversation. "I don't suppose any of us got the number of the car?"

Joe sneered. "Oh, naturally. First thing I thought when she tried to run me down. I really must get the registration number of her car."

Ignoring his cynicism, Brenda seized on his words. "It was a woman, then?"

The question brought Joe up short. "I, er, I never noticed. It's just that with the Robin Hood woman being a… a woman, I just assumed it was the same… woman."

"I wonder how many women there were in that statement."

Sheila's wry observation seemed to relieve the tension. Even Joe smiled as he responded, "You know what I mean."

Sheila became the model of businesslike efficiency. "Yes, well, we'd better get into the hotel and get them to call the police. We need to report this."

"Yeah, and I need to speak to Gemma again."

***

Back in England, Gemma had made her way to the outskirts of Harrogate and was busy talking to Tom Higginshaw in the untidy, unkempt parlour of his farmhouse. She had entered through the kitchen where the old, wooden table was cluttered with pot and dishes, and the sink had been left overflowing with them. The whole place was bathed in that odour of negligence, as if it had not been cleaned in months.

Higginshaw was about forty years of age, tall and stout, causing Gemma to wonder how he had coped with the strenuous efforts required of a builder.

"I weren't always like this, you know." He patted his rotund belly. "All this were muscle and one bit. But I haven't been able to work since the accident, and it's all turned to blubber."

"You're not married, Mr Higginshaw?"

"I am, but not for much longer. She did a runner the minute the money dried up. Been gone three months now. Would you mind telling me what this is all about?"

"No problem. Are you aware that you were under investigation by the North Shires Insurance Company?"

"Aye. I know that middle-aged bint had been watching me. Haven't seen her for a week or three, mind. Her and that little fella followed me all round Harrogate on Saturday afternoon about two months ago."

Gemma's interest piqued. "Little fella?"

"Don't know who he is. A bit of a shortarse. Scrawny too. No meat on him. I saw 'em getting out of a black Ford Ka near the bus station, and every time I turned round that afternoon, they were there. After that, I kept seeing her. Sometimes she was in town, and other times she was out here on the lane, and I figured she was watching me. And if she was watching me, she could only be from North Shires.

33

And then she came to see me, gave me some right hassle. They think I'm scamming them, but I'm not. I can barely walk since the accident."

Gemma had switched off long before Higginshaw finished talking. He had recognised Denise, he had spotted Joe, he knew what kind of car Joe drove, and he knew what they were doing. Moreover, his wife was not here.

Was it enough? The simple answer was, no. She didn't have enough to arrest him on suspicion, let alone think about charges. She needed to get away, drive the thirty or so miles back to Sanford, bring herself up to speed on dates and times, and then come back and challenge him.

She stood up. "Thank you for your time, Mr Higginshaw. I may need to speak to you again, but if so, I'll get the local police to contact you first."

"Hang about. You haven't told me what this is about."

Gemma paused as she retreated to the door. She turned to face him. "Well, Denise Latham, the 'bint' as you describe her, is dead. She was run off the road. And whoever did it may just be after the scrawny little fella… my Uncle Joe. And it's possible that you, and your missing wife, may be in the frame for it."

After the unkempt odour of the place, she felt glad of the fresh, if rainy air, when she climbed into her car. She felt tired and she was the wrong side of Harrogate for an easy ride home. Whether she chose to go through Leeds or head east for the A1, she was faced with a tough drive home.

She fired the engine, turned the car around and as she was pulling out of the gate, her phone rang. She stopped, checked the menu and read, 'Joe'. She made the connection. "These calls must be costing you a fortune, Uncle Joe."

"Yeah, well, you spoke to Gallego yesterday and he said I was off my tree, right?"

"He did."

"There's been another attempt. An hour ago. Right outside the hotel. And this time there was no question. Sheila and Brenda were with me. They saw this woman try to run me down."

34

The news merely served to confirm the suspicion which had been growing in Gemma's mind all day. "I'll speak to Gallego later, when he's had chance to doing a little poking around. In the meantime, Joe, have you heard of a man called Tom Higginshaw? Lives in a rambling, dirty old farmhouse outside Harrogate."

There was a considerable pause, and she could picture Joe's brow creasing as he searched his memory.

"Is it that guy Denise was shadowing a coupla months back?"

"Yes. That's him."

"All right, so I know of him. I never spoke to him."

"You may not have done, but he recognised you and Denise. Do you know how far she got with her investigation? Cos if she found him out, he stood to lose about two million. It strikes me that would be a good enough reason to shut her up… and you."

"Gemma, this is a woman going for me."

"Yes, Joe, and Higginshaw's wife is AWOL."

The announcement brought another short silence on the Majorca end of the connection. "Do you know what she looks like?"

"Do you know what Killington looks like?"

"Nope."

"Snap."

"Listen, Gemma, a lot of Denise's work was confidential, and she didn't always tell me everything. She asked me to go with her that day to try and be more inconspicuous. If she had anything on him, it will be on her laptop. As far as I know Ray Dockerty took it away and to my knowledge, it was never returned. Why would it be? The flat was Denise's. I had to move out virtually the minute she died. But I'm sure Dockerty will have it. She had no family to pass it to.

"Why the hell…" Gemma bit her tongue. The news that one of Leeds' CID's most senior detectives had taken away the laptop sent a flash of anger through her, before she remembered that the incident in which Denise had died happened within Leeds' jurisdiction. She, Gemma, had been involved only as a liaison officer, and only then because of Joe's relationship with the dead woman.

"Gemma? You still there, Gemma?"

"Yeah. Right. Sorry, Joe. Listen, I have to get back to Sanford, but I'll bell Dockerty on my way back, and see if I can't get the laptop from him. I don't see why he needs to keep it anyway. I'll also ring Gallego the minute I'm back in the office, and if you get to know anything more, bell me."

"Will do."

***

If Joe and his friends suspected that Inspector Gallego had been dismissive of their arguments, they were wrong.

A career based in and around Palmanova, Magaluf and Santa Ponsa had seen him deal with English tourists on all levels, from the simple, brutish lager louts, to the genuinely distressed who had suffered at the hands of pickpockets or more violent muggers. He had also handled his fair share of individuals like Joe Murray; people who imagined criminals lurking around every corner, keeping them under surveillance and waiting for the opportunity to strike.

As a result, although he remained circumspect, he was open to the possibility that Murray was right.

After his interview with Anna Squillano, he looked further into her past and decided that she was beyond reproach. If the suspect, the unknown Killington, really was intent upon harming Joe Murray, it was unlikely that she had enlisted the help of the naïve Anna. But she had still needed access to the sun terrace of the Palmanova Corona, which involved securing a silver-coloured wristband such as that worn by all the guests.

Gallego knew the Corona. It was one of the town's better hotels, part of a large, nationwide group, and if they were not always choosy about the guests they accepted they were meticulous when it came to employing staff. Any member of staff found to have been issuing identity bands

36

to non-residents would be instantly dismissed, and it would not make sense for any member of the crew to risk his/her position to let a non-resident in.

But if that were the case, then the member of staff in question must have received a very large pay off, and Gallego had already instituted a check on the financial comings and goings of the hotel staff from the general manager all the way down to the lowest, meanest janitor in the place. He did not expect to find anything untoward.

While waiting for the results he considered other means by which Ms Killington could have secured the wristband, and he had obtained a sample from the hotel's reception desk, where the bands were issued to guests.

It comprised a simple strip of plastic tape, about three quarters of a centimetre wide, punched with holes half a centimetre apart. Wrapped around the wrist it was clipped into place with a press-stud, and any excess tape cut off with scissors. Where, if not at the Corona, would Killington get hold of it?

He drove down into Palmanova, and just before reaching the main square, he turned left, drove along a short distance and parked outside a large, double-fronted shop, its white logo declaring *Ferreteria* in bold, blue letters: what the English would call an ironmongers.

The proprietor, a wizened, sixty-something did not sell them. "You will find them easiest on the internet. Very cheap. Only a few cents each."

Gallego tossed the option around his mind, and dismissed it. Delivery from the internet would take at least a couple of days, especially on an island like Majorca. Killington would have needed advance information on where Murray was staying and inside knowledge of the hotel's practices, procedures and equipment. Although not beyond the bounds of possibility, it was stretching credibility. There was too great a capacity for things to go wrong. Suppose Joe Murray and his friends had cancelled at the last moment? Suppose they had arrived in Palmanova and decided to go to another hotel? No, Killington had to be sure of everything before she secured the wristband.

The proprietor assured him that there was a wholesale hotel supplier in Palma, but it would not be easy for anyone to walk in off the street and buy over the counter.

Coming out of the shop, Gallego sat in his car and engaged the logic circuits of his brain. Minutes later, the obvious solution occurred to him, and he rang the Corona.

"This is Inspector Gallego of the *Policia Nacional*. I'm investigating the incident during an archery competition yesterday. Tell me, do any of your guests ever lose their wristbands?"

"It happens," the clerk replied. "It can be a problem with children, but we have adults lose them, too."

Gallego ended the call. Obviously, he would not be as difficult as he had initially imagined. It was perfectly possible that Killington had found a wristband on the street outside the hotel.

Whether or not Murray was right, Killington had entered the hotel, had taken part in a competition when she was not entitled to, and then disappeared, all of which called into question her motive. It also left Gallego with the problem of where to find her. There was no adequate description of her. No one had taken particular notice, and while the hotel's CCTV covering the entrance and reception, had picked her up, the image was not good. No one, not even Anna, could identify her.

He started the engine, and was about to drive away when his mobile rang. He checked the menu, read 'Palmanova Corona Hotel' and made the connection.

After listening to the frantic, garbled words of the clerk, he killed the connection, jammed the car into gear and shunted the car round before tearing off for the Corona.

Chapter Five

Joe was still in a state of heightened anxiety after speaking to the clerks on reception, one of whom rang Gallego while Joe, Sheila and Brenda were waiting.

From the lobby they made their way out to the sun terrace where the two women promptly called together the other members of the 3rd Age Club.

Taking up a table in the shaded area by the pool bar, Joe, Sheila and Brenda sat to one side; facing them were the Staineses, Les Tanner and Sylvia Goodson, flanked by George Robson and Owen Frickley. With the exception of Sylvia, who kept herself wrapped up in a thin cardigan over her printed dress, all of them were lightly clad in bathing costumes or shorts, ideal for sunbathing.

Drinks were ordered, soft for Joe, Sheila and Sylvia, various alcoholic beverages for the others, and when everyone was settled, Sheila and Brenda outlined the events of the morning and reminded them of the previous day's incident.

"It looks like someone's definitely got it in for you, Joe," George Robson said after taking a healthy swallow of lager. "What you want us to do about it, Brenda?"

Joe wondered why George had directed his question at Brenda when Sheila had obviously taken the central role, but then he recalled that George and Brenda had an on/off, casual relationship.

Brenda had no hesitation in answering. "I want us to babysit him."

The announcement brought a ripple of laughter from the group. Even Joe was forced to smile at the imagery her words generated. But his smile soon faded, replaced with irritable pride.

"I'm not a child. I don't need bloody babysitting."

Sheila disagreed. "I think you do. She's tried twice – if we assume that the driver of the car is this mysterious Killington woman – and next time, she may succeed. We can make it harder for her if we ensure you're never alone."

Joe remained outraged. "Gonna be a bit awkward if I score. What are you gonna do if I'm getting it on with some woman? Bring your video camera with you?"

"That'll be one for the family album," Owen Frickley quipped.

George added to the humour. "I can see the tagline now. Yorkshire chef putting a bun in local girl's oven."

The remark brought a round of risible chuckles from the table and a disapproving 'tut-tut' from Sylvia.

"We do understand the meaning of discretion, Joe," Julia Staines said.

Her husband, Alec, one of Joe's closest friends, reinforced his wife's opinion. "It's not about invading your privacy, but making sure you don't come to any harm. I think Sheila and Brenda are right. What kind of friends are we if we don't look after you?"

Joe was secretly grateful for their concern, but he made another half-hearted protest. "I'm perfectly capable of looking after myself."

This caused another bout of laughter from the table, and it was left to Les Tanner to remind Joe, "You were never any use in a fight, Murray. When we were all at school, the girls used to beat you up. The intervening fifty years haven't improved your ability to defend yourself."

"I am not frightened of this woman."

"Nobody says you are." Sheila took his hand. "Be practical. She has the element of surprise, she's very probably a good few years younger than you, and if she goes for you again, you'll need an extraordinarily lucky punch to put her down. Now stop being silly, Joe. I'm sure we can protect you, without impinging on our holiday more than she already has."

Brenda took up the initiative. "The question is how do we go about it? I think Joe is safe enough with Sheila and me while we're out and about, but we can't be with him every minute of the day, especially when we're out here on the sun terrace."

"Nights are out for me and George," Owen said. "While you lot are hanging round this dump, we're boogying the night away in the town."

George nodded his agreement while taking another mouthful of lager. Putting the near-empty glass back on the table, he drew a deep breath. "But we can watch out while we're here."

"When we're not sleeping it off."

The remark from Owen could have sparked a fresh round of ribald debate, but at that moment Inspector Gallego arrived and after introducing himself to those people who did not know him, drew Sheila, Brenda and Joe off to one side, where he spent the next ten minutes taking statements from them.

When he was finished he spent a few moments reading through the statements before delivering his verdict.

"I can see where you might think this is another attack, Señor Murray, but as in the last, er, happening, there is nothing to say that this really was an attempt to kill or injure you. It could well have been a driver in a hurry and not paying attention."

This brought a babble of protest from Joe and the two women, against which Gallego held up a hand to silence them.

"However, I have to consider the possibility that you are right, and I will take my investigations forward with that in mind. I must now leave you all and try to trace this car. I will come back to you with any news as soon as I have it, and if anything else happens please get in touch."

He stood, and with a formal half-bow, turned and marched stiffly away.

"A chocolate teapot," Joe grumbled. "What has to happen before he'll take me seriously? Does this lunatic

41

actually have to kill me?"

Brenda pouted and looked into the air as if she were seriously considering the question. "Not kill. Injure perhaps."

"Bog off."

Following Gallego's example, Joe got to his feet, but instead of leaving the hotel he marched to the safety barrier and looked out over Palmanova Bay, seeking peace in the gentle bobbing of boats on the calm waters.

"Life losing its shine, Joe?"

He'd already sensed a presence alongside him, and he turned to find Julia Staines at his right shoulder.

About the same age as him, in her mid to late-fifties, she was an outstandingly attractive woman, and many years previously, back in their youth, Joe had hankered after a serious relationship with her, but even then he had realised that Alec Staines presented a much better prospect. He was taller, and in better physical shape than Joe, and as a self-employed painter and decorator, he was able to offer Julia a similar, prospective income and the security that went with it, but without actually living on the job, as Joe did in the old Lazy Luncheonette.

"Any attraction life had for me, Julia, disappeared when Denise was killed, and my biggest problem right now is getting people to listen to me."

Julia rested her left hand on his right as they leaned on the barrier. "We're all here for you. I know that that's not much consolation, but…" She trailed off, and he guessed she was having trouble putting her thoughts into words.

He delivered a wrinkled grin. "If I were thirty years younger and bigger than Alec—"

"I'd be thirty years older than you."

***

Back in Sanford, with the time coming up to five thirty, Gemma agreed with Joe.

She had spoken to Gallego, listened to his account of

42

events in Majorca, and accepted his slightly circumspect opinions, but all her instincts and an ingrained knowledge of Joe's astute

thought processes told her that her uncle was indeed, in danger.

Not that she blamed Gallego for his approach. There was, as far as she could judge, little hard evidence, and Palmanova was the kind of resort that was popular with the British, which meant the inspector probably had a lot more on his plate than unsubstantiated attempts on the life of another Brit.

Normally, she could rely upon Joe to arrive at a logically deduced conclusion, but in his current state of mind, grieving for Denise Latham, he was unlikely to be at his most perceptive. It was up to her, to see if she could narrow down the possibilities at this end.

A brief conversation with Ray Dockerty in Leeds secured an appointment with him for ten o'clock the following morning, and the superintendent assured her that the laptop in question would be dredged from the evidence room. In the meantime, failing any further communication from Majorca, there was little else she could do.

She was getting her belongings together when Oughton stepped into her office. A few minutes of amiable, inconsequential chat followed, at the end of which the superintendent asked, "Have you considered Kilburn-Corbin?"

"They're both still inside, sir."

"Yes, I know they are, but their wives were released some time ago, and I know that Kilburn's wife is in Sanford Hospice. Is it possible that Killington is related to her? After all, when Joe helped send her husband to prison for life, he ruined all their plans, and I think Jan Kilburn might have wanted revenge. Obviously, she can't deal with the matter herself but she may have relatives trying to do it for her. Or even a sister so angry with what's happened to Jan that she's prepared to go for Joe."

Gemma, convinced that she had a better lead in Tom

Higginshaw, doubted it, but in the interests of efficiency, she thought it worth following up, and ten minutes later, she pulled out of the car park at the rear of the police station, and joined the post-rush hour traffic moving out of Sanford.

Her route would normally take her along Leeds Road to the flat she shared with her partner, but instead of heading west, she turned northeast on Wetherby Road, and headed out into the more rural outskirts of town, when she eventually turned into the placid, calming lawns and gardens of Sanford Hospice, where, after some discussion with the senior manager, she was eventually shown to the single room housing Janet Kilburn.

Her husband, Bradley, along with his accomplice, Alan Corbin, and had been sentenced to life, with a minimum term of twenty-five years for several murders. Janet and Corbin's wife, Melanie, had been given eighteen months for aiding and abetting. The hospice manager explained that Janet had been released early suffering from lung cancer, and moved to end-of-life care, where she had remained for the last ten months.

Gemma remembered her from her court appearance; a smartly dressed, good looking, if hard-faced woman of about forty-five, with a neatly coiffeured shower of blonde hair. She bore no resemblance to the shell of a woman permanently bedridden, oxygen tubes in her nose to help her breathe, her skin wrinkled and decaying, hair mostly gone – a result of chemotherapy, Gemma guessed – drip feeds in her arm, and barely able to speak.

Gemma was there for half an hour, but achieved little. Janet denied that she had any relatives named Killington and she had had no contact with Melanie Corbin since her transfer from prison – something the hospice manager later confirmed. She wanted to know why Gemma was asking, and when she heard the explanation she gave a weak laugh which dissolved into a coughing fit.

"If someone's trying to kill Murray, good for them. I'll see him on the other side and give him hell for the rest of eternity."

Gemma came away from the hospice at about seven fifteen, and considered the visit a waste of her valuable time. Even if Janet were involved, she was never going to say so. It was left to her, Gemma, and the efforts of Inspector Gallego, Joe, Sheila and Brenda, and the other members of the 3rd Age Club to track down the wannabe assassin and stop her.

***

Joe woke suddenly, and for a moment struggled to recognise his surroundings. This was not Denise's flat, and it was not Brenda's spare room, where he was currently living.

The logic and memory circuits clicked into place and the room took on the familiar layout of a single bed studio in the Palmanova Corona Hotel.

He had returned to his room at half past four, and promptly hit the bed for a much needed afternoon nap. The LED display of his travel clock, a small, grey cube which had seen many years' service, registered just after six. He had slept longer than he intended. He was due to meet the girls at seven o'clock in the dining room, and he still needed to shower, shave and dress for the evening.

He rolled from the bed and padded across the room and out onto the balcony, overlooking the bay and beach down in Palmanova. It was his policy to take a short nap every afternoon and then spend an hour on the balcony enjoying a cup of tea and pottering with his netbook, downloading the day's photographs from his compact digital camera, making notes in his journal, usually an account of the day's events, his thoughts and feelings.

Time was tight. He would probably have to cut short most of that process. But he would not do without his cup of tea.

He turned back into the room, filled the kettle and switched it on. He got a cup and saucer ready – two sugars, and a tea bag, milk to come last, when he had added water and stirred – and then moved to the wardrobe from which he took his attire for the evening; a pair of beige, casual trousers, and a pale blue, short-sleeved shirt.

From there he retrieved his towel from the balcony rail, where he had left it to air, and then made his way towards the bathroom.

He didn't get that far. Moving through the room he spotted a sheet of notepaper which had been folded in half and pushed under the door. It was probably from Sheila or Brenda, another effort to reassure him that they were there, looking out for him. He was grateful, of course, but it was getting out of hand, and he hated mollycoddling.

Dropping the towel on the bed, he strode to the door and picked up the note. He unfolded it, read its short message, and his features paled.

NEXT TIME MURRAY NEXT TIME

Chapter Six

The sun rose promising another hot and sunny day in Palmanova, and Inspector Gallego arrived at nine fifteen, after the hotel had rung him at eight thirty.

With Joe in a state of high anxiety, the note had been the sole topic of conversation during dinner and throughout the previous evening's entertainment, which amounted to several games of bingo and a young couple with half a dozen trained, performing parrots.

"Not exactly a West End show," Joe had complained when he stepped out for a cigarette.

Alec Staines and Les Tanner went with him. Les was a dedicated pipe smoker whereas Alec, like Joe, was a long-time cigarette man. Unlike Joe, he had never stopped, and he, along with everyone else, was surprised to find Joe smoking again.

"Daft, I know, but with all this happening, I need a stressbuster, and the tobacco's doing it."

"Talking of all that's happening, Murray, are you any closer to identifying this woman?"

Les Tanner was in the habit of referring to Joe by his surname. A former captain in the Territorial Army, now a senior administrator with Sanford Borough Council, he called almost everyone by their surname, and Joe had long-ago ceased to take offence at it. As far as he was concerned, it was a part of life's rich tapestry.

"I spoke to Gemma this afternoon, and she's checking up on some muppet from Harrogate."

Alec found that amusing. "Not many professional hitmen in Harrogate." He put on an imaginary upper-class accent. "They bring down the tone of the neighbourhood, don't you know."

Joe snorted. "This guy's a builder. You might know him, Alec. Tom Higginshaw."

Alec took a long drag on his cigarette. "Doesn't ring any bells. Mind, it wouldn't. I'm a painter. I don't do much site work. My job tends to start when the brickies, roofers, plumbers and chippies have all gone home. One man band, is he?"

Joe shrugged. "I don't know anything about him… but Denise did, and it makes me wonder about the accident that killed her."

The entire evening passed in the same vein, and when they returned to their rooms Joe was escorted all the way to his door, despite his protests that he would be all right.

It had been the same at breakfast, when Sheila rang him as he was dressing, and ordered him not to leave his room until she and Brenda knocked on the door.

"I feel like I've been put into the witness protection programme," he complained as they accompanied him to the dining room.

His companions would hear none of it, and he noticed that one or other stayed by his side during the meal, even when he went to the servery to select his food.

Gallego swung too far in the opposite direction for Joe's liking.

While he was happy to take away the offending note and subject it to routine but unspecified forensic tests, he still refused to accept it as definitive proof that Joe was under threat.

"For all we know, Señor, it could be one of your English practical jokes."

"It's not funny," Joe complained, "and none of my friends would do this."

"I do not suggest your friends. I think perhaps others in the hotel have heard of these rumours, and they may be leading you on."

Joe fumed. "What will it take to convince you?"

"Something more than this, Señor. Think about what has

happened so far. A stray arrow misses you, a car misses you and you have received a threatening note. For someone who is trying to kill you, Ms Killington is a terrible shot, even with a car, is she not? And even this note looks as if it was written in lipstick."

The summary did not to assuage Joe's anger. "The British police—"

"Would do exactly as I do, Señor Murray. They may, perhaps, put a guard on you. I do not have the manpower to do that. Therefore I ask the hotel to keep an eye out for strangers, and I ask you to take care of your safety, and report anything to me which happens." Gallego held up the note, now enclosed in an evidence bag. "And this, you have done. But you have not yet told me what this woman looks like. No one has. A general call to the hotels in Palmanova and Magaluf and Santa Ponsa has not brought this woman out of the shade and into the sun. I am sorry, but I do not have a huge team of detectives I can call upon to investigate what appears to be nothing worse than a bad joke put out by a foolish woman." He held up the note again. "I will report my findings on this."

With a curt yet polite nod he turned smartly on his heel and took his leave.

***

While the sun shone on the Balearic Islands, it was not so generous to the city of Leeds.

When Gemma arrived at Millgarth Police station for a ten o'clock appointment with Detective Superintendent Raymond Dockerty, the sky was sullen, overcast and threatening rain driven by a stiff, easterly wind, and she was glad to get inside.

After presenting her warrant card to reception, she was shown to Dockerty's office on the third floor, where the big man greeted her with a warm handshake and friendly smile.

"Good to see you again, Gemma, even if it is under trying circumstances." He laughed as he waved her into the

49

visitor's chair opposite. "But that seems to be the hallmark of our meetings, doesn't it?"

Gemma returned a weak smile. She had not forgotten the days when Joe had been suspected of murder, and the manner in which Dockerty had effectively reduced her to carrying out work which would normally have been the province of a detective constable.

She made an effort to suppress her irritability. "It's good to see you too, sir."

Dockerty relaxed, half turning his chair so he could look one way at her and the others through the windows. "So, what's this about Denise Latham's laptop?"

As briefly as she could, Gemma related her inquiries of the previous day, and outlined her suspicions. "I have to stress, sir, that I have absolutely no evidence to suggest that Higginshaw was involved in Denise's death. I don't even know that Higginshaw is trying to scam the insurance company, but even the Spanish police are beginning to suspect that Joe is being targeted. When I spoke to Joe yesterday, he was the one who suggested Denise's laptop. If she had uncovered any evidence at all that Higginshaw was pulling a fast one, it will be on that machine. What I'd like to do, with your permission, is take the laptop away and go through the files, see what, if anything, I can uncover."

The superintendent drummed the fingers of his left hand on the desk, then suddenly turned to face her again. "The inquiry into the accident is our case, Gemma, not yours. We asked you to liaise with Joe. As far as we're concerned it was a hit and run, and we've made precious little progress in tracking down the other vehicle. I'll grant your request, and you can take the machine away, but I want it clearly understood that if you find anything, it comes back to me. I don't want you, or North Yorkshire taking over the inquiry. Understand?"

It was exactly what Gemma had expected. "Yes, sir, but I assume you'll credit my role in the investigation."

He smiled broadly. "I like police officers with one eye on their future. Have you ever considered a transfer to

50

Leeds? You'd be more than welcome on my team."

Gemma laughed. "Thank you, sir, but for the moment I'm quite happy in Sanford."

Dockerty reached for the phone. "Well, the offer's there when you're ready to change your mind. Let me get that laptop for you."

***

Back in Palmanova the day dragged on with its usual level of indolence. The Sanford 3rd Age Club broiled in the sun, occasionally turning over to toast the opposite side, scuttling for shade now and then, seeking respite from the heat, in the seating near the pool bar.

They stayed together as a group always ensuring that no fewer than two people stayed with Joe at all times, and he found it irritating in the extreme. Yet, he recognised their concern for his safety, and as the day moved on he felt less and less anxious, less inclined to look around seeking this mysterious Killington woman.

Here in Majorca, he was out of his depth, out of his natural element. His forte was observation coupled to logical deduction, and it usually applied to other people, not himself. There was nothing and no one to observe. Lacking an adequate description of Killington there was little point in studying the guests: she could be any one of them. But somehow, he doubted it. Anna, wandering round the area looking for younger people to take part in the water polo match, would recognise Killington in an instant, and hadn't he already been told that the woman was not staying at the Palmanova Corona?

And yet, she had managed to gain access not once but twice, the first time to grab the bow and arrow, the second to push the note under his door.

He knew from experience that such manoeuvres were not difficult. A busy hotel, people coming and going all the time, it was easy to slip in unnoticed and mingle with crowds of holidaymakers. But as he thought about it, how did she know that he, Joe Murray, or indeed, the Sanford 3rd Age Club would be staying at the Palmanova Corona? It could not possibly be coincidence that she was here at the same time. She must have followed them.

He put the question to his two companions.

"You dealt with the booking, Brenda. You're the one who's pally with the travel agent in Sanford."

Brenda, on the verge of nodding off to sleep, sat up instead. "I am, Joe, but Phyllis would never give out details on clients. I know her. I've known her years and she understands confidentiality."

Sheila confirmed it. "Phyllis and I were in secretarial college together forty years ago, and she is the model of business efficiency."

"But she's only one of the staff there isn't she? What about the others?" Joe had been reclining, half-propped up on his lounger. To make his point, he sat upright, swung his feet to the tiles and faced them. "Let's make some assumptions, eh? Let's assume this is for real and not a figment of my imagination as Gallego thinks. And let's imagine this woman has already killed Denise and now she wants me—"

"Now there's a thought, Joe," Brenda interrupted. "Suppose she killed Denise as a love rival and she wants your body."

"It could happen," Sheila teased.

"If she's madly in love with me, she's got an odd way of showing it. You don't tend to shoot your lovers with a bow and arrow, or try to run them down in the middle of the street. Get real, will you?"

"Then what are you driving at?" Brenda demanded. "Come on. I don't have all day. I have some serious sleeping to do."

"She killed Denise in Leeds. She's followed us here to get at me. How did she know we were coming here? And even if one of the members told her we were going to Majorca, how did she know which hotel we'd be staying at? And don't tell me she went round them all looking for us, because I don't believe it. She knew where we would be."

The women remained silent. Sheila raised her hands and let them fall into her lap as a gesture of defeat. Brenda sucked cola through a straw.

Triumphantly, Joe said, "I'll tell you how. Someone at that bloody travel agents told her."

Brenda shook her head and put down her glass. "I don't accept that."

"No?" Joe was equally determined. "Well, let's set someone the job of finding out, huh?" he picked up his mobile and dialled.

***

The Sanford Travel Agency stood in the centre of a dour parade of shops on Bargate, a narrow street just off Market Square. It was one of the older parts of the town centre, a hangover from the days when, aside from a few big, High Street names, like Woolworths and Lewis's, all shops tended to be local.

Leaving her car at the police station a few streets way, Gemma wondered just how well supported these shops were, but as she stepped in, glad to be out of the heavy, spring rain, the staff uniforms reminded her that, although the place was still known as Sanford Travel Agency, it was owned by one of the major players.

It was three o'clock local time when she put Joe's question to Phyllis Edison, the manager, who greeted her with the smile of a salesperson. It quickly changed to that of a battle-hardened businesswoman when Phyllis promptly denied the prospect with all the force of character so typical of Sanford women.

"No way at all. My staff would never discuss another client with anyone. The first thing I drill into them is confidentiality, and it's constantly reinforced at our weekly training sessions. I selected each and every one of these girls myself, Inspector, and I guarantee that not one of them would do such a thing, and I don't care what Joe Murray has to say."

Waiting for the tirade to burn itself out, Gemma reflected on Phyllis's use of Joe's name. He was known throughout the town. Many people admired him, just as many – and for the moment she would include Phyllis Edison in that number for the simple reason that she used his full name, rather than referring to him as 'Joe' – disliked him, but everyone knew him, knew of his foibles and his intuitive mind.

"Mrs Edison, Joe's life is under threat. Some woman has followed him – and the rest of the 3rd Age Club – to Majorca, and we need to work out how she learned where they were staying."

"Then I suggest you talk to members of the club. It's a clever idea, an organisation dedicated to helping the middle-aged and elderly enjoy life, but it's filled with some of the biggest gossips in Sanford."

Since she knew most of the members, Gemma could not disagree with Phyllis's analysis. "It can't have been one of them… well, it could have been, but a good number of them are over there with Joe right now, and he'll be questioning them. I'm handling the Sanford end of the inquiry, and if we can't clear this up, I will drag each of your staff to the station if I have to, and take statements from them."

Phyllis snapped to her feet. "Very well. Let's find out." She marched stiff-backed from the office and out into the shop.

There were no customers. One young woman was busy tidying up the racks of brochures, and another was busy penning out advertisement cards for the special offers displayed in the windows. Two more women were working at their computers, and behind a pane of reinforced, probably bulletproof glass, a teller was cashing up her foreign currency.

Phyllis clapped her hands for attention. "Listen up everyone. Did any of you give away details of the hotel where the Sanford 3rd Age Club are staying?"

Although they all turned to focus on her, none of them

reacted. Behind the currency desk, the teller ignored everything and carried on counting her pounds, euros, and dollars.

Phyllis turned a smug face on Gemma, but as she did so, a young blonde woman at the far end of the service desks raised a timid hand. Gemma returned the smug smile and Phyllis rounded on the girl.

"Have we not discussed this often enough, Lindsey? Have I not made it clear—"

Gemma interrupted. "That's enough, Mrs Edison. Lindsey, could you tell me what happened?"

The girl appeared near to tears. "It was about a week ago. This woman came in and said she had a friend in the Sanford 3rd Age Club and she knew they were going away, but she'd forgotten which hotel they were staying in."

"So you told her?" Phyllis fumed.

"Please, Mrs Edison." Gemma smiled encouragement at Lindsey. "Go on."

"I told her we couldn't give out that kind of information and she started getting all worried and nearly crying. She'd promised to see her friend in Majorca and now she couldn't because…" A note of pleading came into Lindsey's voice. "I felt sorry for her, and I didn't think it'd do any harm."

"Well, it has," Phyllis declared, "And I will speak to you personally on this matter."

"Again, Mrs Edison, you can deal with that later. Right now, I need to know about this woman." Gemma concentrated on the assistant again. "Did she give you a name?"

"Killingholme or something like that."

"Killington?"

"Coulda been."

"Could you describe her?"

Lindsey thought about it. "Not tall. Shorter than you. Blonde. thirty-summat, I guess. That's it."

"Well-dressed?"

"Not really. Well, tidy, I suppose, but nothing I'd wear. Boring y'know. Not fashionable."

Gemma turned to Phyllis. "Do you have CCTV?"

"Yes, but it's focused on the currency desk. Unless she bought currency here, she wouldn't be on it."

Turning back to Lindsey, Gemma pressed for more details. "It's too much to hope that she actually booked the hotel or even a flight with you, I suppose?"

The young woman shook her head and with a sulky, cautious eye on Phyllis, replied, "She said she had to go to the bank and get the money, but she'd be back in an hour to book. She never came back."

Again Gemma addressed Phyllis. "Thank you for your help. I don't think Lindsey can help me any further."

"No. But if she wants to help herself, she'd better start listening."

Chapter Seven

"All right, so we know how she found you. That doesn't get us any closer to knowing who she is."

Listening to Sheila state the obvious, Joe's mind drifted. Gemma had telephoned at about half past four, Majorca time, and told him of her findings at the Sanford Travel Agency, and ever since he passed the news on, there had been no other topic for discussion. He was beginning to find it boring.

The Palmanova Corona was typical of most all-inclusive hotels. The dining room was open from seven until nine thirty in the evening, but most guests arrived on the dot at seven o'clock, and the place was crowded.

The food was excellent, but there was a marked lack of variety which, in his opinion, brought the place down to a level similar to his own Lazy Luncheonette. His was a truckers' café, and lorry drivers tended to seek the same food no matter where they stopped for their breaks. In a holiday hotel with a 4-star rating from the local tourist board, Joe expected a greater choice of dishes, and yet the place appeared determined to serve up the standard, and basic, cheap and cheerful English meals: fish and chips, sausage and chips, burger and chips. There were alternatives. Chicken Andaluz, for example, and paella, but they were poorly labelled, for which reason they were not popular.

"I think Gemma is onto something with that builder. Did you get to see the builder's wife, Joe?"

Brenda's question brought him back from his thoughts on the catering. "What? Oh. No. I only got a glimpse of Higginshaw himself, never mind his missus." He pushed his plate to one side, finished with the veal and overcooked vegetables, and took a sip of house red. "It doesn't make much sense to me. Higginshaw might have guessed who we were but shining Denise on and trying to bump me off won't save his two million quid."

And Brenda had finished her meal and in deference to her greater appetite took a much larger swallow of the wine. "So, come on, Sherlock. Who is it, then?"

"The sixty-four dollar question." Joe's brow furrowed.

Sheila eyed the service counter. "To pudding or not to pudding. That is the question." She concentrated on Joe. "Who else would have reason to attack both you and Denise?" Her eyes roamed back to the food on offer. "Perhaps a dish of fruit salad."

Joe was not ready to let her get away so easily. "You have to remember that Denise was driving my car when she was killed. I still believe that Killington thought I was at the wheel when she ran the car off the road. If I'm right, it means I was the target, and Higginshaw can't possibly be responsible. We need to look at other suspects."

Brenda pushed back her chair and stood up. "I'm with Sheila. Pudding first, murderers after. You want anything while I'm at the counter?"

Joe shook his head and the two women went off to the dessert.

Left alone with his thoughts, Joe ran through a mental catalogue of women who might want him dead. In the space of a few seconds he had half a dozen on the list, and three of those had been convicted of murder. He eliminated them immediately. They were still in prison. As the list grew, he added those who had been sentenced for lesser offences; manslaughter, aiding and abetting, conspiracy, attempts to pervert the course of justice. He had no idea how many of them were still inside, out on licence, or had served their sentences and been released.

Not for the first time he wished he were home where all the information he needed would be to hand.

"We understand where you're coming from," Sheila said

when he expanded on his theory, "but you shouldn't dismiss Higginshaw so quickly. His wife is unaccounted for, and until that changes, he – and she – are possibles."

Joe left it at that and excusing himself, left the dining room to step outside for a smoke.

With the time coming up to eight o'clock the sun had dipped towards the western horizon, and hung in the sky just above the hills, a blazing orb casting a crimson glow across the calm waters of the bay and the surrounding land. Down in the town the first lights had come on in the bars, restaurants, and hotels. Soon, with the coming of night, Palmanova would burst into life. Hen parties, stag parties, revellers of all nationalities (but mainly British) would come out ready to burn off energy in an orgy of drinking and dancing, singing and smooching.

He wondered idly how many young women would wake tomorrow morning and anxiously reach for the pregnancy testing kit. How many young, betrothed men and women would greet the new day lying alongside a stranger of the opposite sex? Unlike many of his peers and contemporaries, Joe did not disapprove. These youngsters were at the age where life was to be enjoyed. They lived in the here and now, and they would worry about tomorrow when tomorrow came.

Had he been so different when he was their age? No. It was true to say that in a working class backwater like Sanford, foreign holidays were unheard of back then. In his youth, it was Blackpool, Mablethorpe and Torquay, rather than Benidorm, Majorca, or Torremolinos, but the principle was the same. You're a long time dead so get out and enjoy life while you can.

He recalled waking on the hard floor of a police cell in Skegness. George Robson was snoring on one of the concrete slabs that passed for a bed, Owen Frickley was on the other, and all three had been locked up for being drunk and disorderly. How many young men and women mingling in the street lights in Palmanova would find themselves in the same position tomorrow morning?

Live now. Let tomorrow hang.

Joe reflected that he didn't have many more tomorrows to come. Even fewer, if Killington had her way.

As his thoughts turned in this gloomy direction, he suddenly realised he was alone. For all their determination to ensure his safety, the 3rd Age Club had forgotten about him.

A sly smile crept across his face. Like a prisoner suddenly aware of an opening, he decided to make a break for it.

***

"YES!"

A triumphant Gemma shouted the word at the empty room. She had Higginshaw banged to rights. He was trying to scam the insurance company.

Denise, as befitted a former detective sergeant, had done a first-class job of investigating the builder. She had kept him under surveillance for over a week, discreetly following him wherever he went (including the day she had taken Joe with her) and monitored him from the lane outside his farmhouse, from which vantage point she had taken several videos.

The footage could not be considered definitive proof of anything, but it clearly showed Higginshaw carrying out occasional, heavy tasks which he said he was incapable of. Simple things like climbing a ladder to clean the windows, pottering in the garden and then moving what appeared to be heavy wheelbarrow full of the usual garden detritus. Higginshaw may have been injured, but he was not as bad as he made out, and Denise made that clear in her case notes, copies of which Gemma hoped she had deposited with North Shires.

The final video and the last note she made were both dated two weeks before Denise was killed, and it seems significant to Gemma that there was no mention of Higginshaw's wife, but then again Higginshaw had insisted she had left him before Denise's investigation got under way.

Was that true? Gemma had no way of knowing, but she knew how to find out.

Outside, night was falling upon Sanford and she knew her next move would not be popular, but at a pinch she could always lay blame at Superintendent Dockerty's door. Hadn't he told her to keep him informed?

She picked up the telephone and dialled the North Yorkshire police in Harrogate, asking to be put through to CID.

Over the next ten minutes she outlined the situation to a Detective Constable Lacey, the duty officer, and notwithstanding his complaints – respectfully phrased in deference to her rank – she received an assurance that Higginshaw would be brought in for questioning first thing in the morning, to which she replied that she would travel to Harrogate to interrogate the builder.

"I'm particularly interested in the whereabouts of his wife. I have a suspicion she may be guilty of murder and we need to find her as soon as we can. You understand?"

"Perfectly, ma'am," came the weary response.

Cutting the connection, Gemma next phoned Joe, but getting no answer she tried Sheila instead.

"Hello, Mrs Riley. It's Gemma Craddock. I've been trying to get hold of Uncle Joe, but he's not answering."

Sheila sounded on the verge of panic. "We can't get him either, and we can't find him. He's disappeared, Gemma. Vanished into thin air."

***

At the Palmanova Corona the air was thick with worry and recrimination.

Calling a meeting of the 3rd Age Club on the open deck of the upper lounge bar, Sheila told them of the discovery she and Brenda had made.

Although they disapproved, they had thought nothing of

61

it when Joe had disappeared for a cigarette. It was only when he didn't return after half an hour that they began to worry, and as twilight fell they scoured the hotel looking for him. He was not in the dining room, he was not in any of the three bars and when they checked his room they got no answer. More worried than ever they inquired at reception, but none of the clerks had noticed him leaving the hotel.

It took a long time but eventually they managed to persuade the duty manager that Joe could be in some danger, for which reason they needed to check his room. Protesting that it could be construed as an invasion of a guest's privacy, the manager eventually capitulated but only after Sheila and Brenda agreed to accept full responsibility.

"Do you think it's worth switching on the video camera on my phone?" Brenda asked as they hurried along the corridor towards Joe's room.

"Whatever for?" Sheila asked with a feeling that she already knew the answer.

"Catching Joe at it with a woman might be useful when we come to ask for a pay rise."

Sheila suppressed the urge to smile. The situation was too worrying for humour.

Joe was not in his room. None of his belongings had been removed, and when they checked the safe, they found it open and empty.

"That doesn't mean anything," Sheila said. "Joe doesn't use the room safes when he's on holiday. He doesn't trust them. He keeps his passport and money with him at all times." She turned anxiously to Brenda. "Perhaps he's just gone for a walk."

Brenda, who beneath her humour could not hide her own unease, forced a smile. "Maybe he really has trapped off with some woman, and they've gone to her room instead."

Sheila checked her watch. "It's not nine o'clock yet. A bit early for shenanigans."

This time Brenda's sly grin was genuine. "Take it from an expert, it is never too early for shenanigans."

After reporting to the 3rd Age Club, Sheila laced into

them.

"We were supposed to be looking out for Joe, and as bodyguards, we are simply appalling. And I don't exclude myself from that."

Alec Staines tried to inject a note of optimism. "He'll be all right, Sheila. Joe always comes out on top."

"To my knowledge, Alec, this is the first time he's ever been faced with a homicidal maniac."

"There was that time at your place," Brenda said, reminding her of an incident some years previously when Sheila had been faced with a shotgun-wielding, serial killer.

"That's true, but it was me facing a homicidal maniac. Joe came in to help." Sheila appealed to the group as a whole. "Joe is our friend. We can't rely on the local police to protect him. It's up to us to do it."

Les Tanner raised a hand. "Allow me to make a suggestion." He got to his feet so everyone could see and hear him. "Murray is not in the hotel, so the chances are he's gone down into the town. Knowing him, he's probably gone looking for this woman. Robson and Frickley are down there, too. Why don't we telephone them and ask them to keep an eye out for him? You know those two. We've been here four days and they know every pub in the town. If anyone can find him, it's them, and we could ask them to ring you, Sheila, or you, Brenda, when they find him so that we can make arrangements to go down and bring him back here… or at the very least stay with him for the rest of the evening."

It was the logical answer, Sheila realised, and after thanking Tanner, she drifted into the background allowing Brenda to lead the discussion while she phoned George Robson.

Five minutes later she was back with the group. "George and Owen are on the case… although I don't know how much use that'll be. Apparently, the centre of Palmanova is packed."

***

If the club members had any problem imagining the town from Sheila's description, Joe would have understood at once.

Of walking along the main street, *Carrer Cala Blanca*, towards the junction where the *Eastenders*, the *Prince William* and *Cutty Sark* formed a triangle of attractive, British-themed bars, the pavements were packed with young and old, all determined to enjoy the night.

Shorts and T-shirts, and many of them bearing the logos of famous football clubs, or other, familiar British icons such as the Union Jack, were the main order of the day, interspersed with more sensible attire, skirts and blouses, casual trousers and shirts, even the occasional cardigan, mostly worn by the middle-aged or elderly holidaymakers.

The street was a cacophony of raw noise, the jabber of conversation emanating from the shops, bars and passers-by backed up by the loud and irritating music from the various establishments. Some of it was recorded, but most of it came from karaoke in the different bars, and the vocals, whether crooned, screeched or bawled, formed an incomprehensible blether, as alien to Joe's ears as one of the locals rattling in his native Spanish tongue.

He was not concerned for his safety. There were hundreds of people out here, and anyone foolish enough to attack him would probably find themselves buried in a welter of bodies before they could inflict any serious damage.

He was a man with a mission; to root out this woman who, he was convinced, had wrecked and now threatened his life.

His phone had rung several times, and it was always Sheila or Brenda. He had not answered for good reasons. First, he doubted that he would hear what they were saying. Amongst all the street noise, he had not actually heard the phone ring. He had felt it vibrating in his shirt pocket. Beyond that, he knew that if he spoke to them they would make a determined effort to bring him back to the comparative safety of the hotel. He had had enough of the cocoon in which they had enshrouded him. He had had enough of cowering away, hiding from this would-be assassin. It was time to take the initiative, put himself out and about, in the open, invite her to come for him again, smoke her out where he could see and identify her.

And if she did not come tonight? Then he would be here again tomorrow, and the night after, and he would continue to be here, even when 'here' meant Sanford, until he had her.

To some extent, he was still in a passive position. He had only the vaguest description of her, and amongst these crowds he would be unlikely to recognise her. She would have to take action, and only then would he know. It was at the forefront of his mind as he called in this bar, that pub, those shops.

She could, he realised, be anyone, anywhere. He could have been standing next to her when he ambled into *The Prince William*. He could have stared her in the eye amongst the crowds watching football in *The Cutty Sark*. He would not know, but as he left those places he kept one eye over his shoulder for signs of anyone, particularly a woman, following him.

He walked up the short rise opposite *The Cutty Sark*, past crowded tables outside the *Cock & Bull*, and stepped into the pub through the side entrance.

It was jam-packed with bodies. The bar was practically invisible behind a sea of people clamouring for drinks. Every seat in the house was taken, and groups of men and women were dotted in all corners of the room. Upon a makeshift stage a young woman, wearing only a pair of tight shorts, and a skimpy bikini top was squawking into the karaoke microphone. Joe had an idea that she was supposed to be singing *I Will Always Love You*, but she was so drunk that the words were unintelligible.

Scanning the crowds again, seeking anyone who might resemble the slender description Anna had given them, he thought he saw George Robson and Owen Frickley amongst the crowds at the bar.

A wry smile crossed his lips. This was their kind of place. Both had been married, both were divorced, both enjoyed the freedom their unattached lives brought them. Joe, too, was divorced, but he had responsibility for his business and the people who worked for him. George and Owen were employees of Sanford Borough Council, and neither had any such encumbrances. Joe envied them. They lived the same wild life he had been thinking of earlier, and as local authority employees, that life came complete with bulletproof pensions.

He came out into the night again, and while standing on the pavement, surrounded by the overspill from the pub, he debated with himself which way to go next. Surely if this woman were looking for him, she would be out and about right now?

He heard the sound of a scuffle behind him. It was followed by protests and a scream of, "YOU'RE DEAD MEAT, MURRAY."

Joe turned and his colour drained. She was bearing down on him like an express train, the broad blade of a chef's kitchen knife in her right hand. Joe's heart pounded, urging him to run, but he was frozen into immobility, hypnotised by the glint of the steel blade.

Behind her, the men and women she had shoved out of her way were recovering. They would not react fast enough to save him, and Joe knew he was, as she had put it, dead meat.

He raised an arm to ward her off. It was a reflex action, and even as he carried it out, he knew it would do no good. He was at her mercy.

As she bore down on him, there was a blur of movement in the corner of his right eye. "Look out, Joe."

A beefy hand grabbed him by the shirt collar and yanked him out of the way, but in doing so, George Robson put himself in her line of attack and the blade sank into his shoulder.

"Bitch," George cursed as he sank to his knees.

She released the knife and ran off.

Stunned, Owen could only gape. Joe looked down at George, now prone on the ground, then up at Owen, and finally, down the street at her disappearing into the crowds.

"Look out for George, Owen."

And with that, Joe, too, ran off down the street.

Chapter Eight

Despite the Mediterranean sun casting its welcoming balm across the whole island, the day was overcast with personal gloom for Sheila, Brenda and the members of the Sanford 3rd Age Club.

The first they had heard of the incident outside *The Cock & Bull* was a frantic call from Owen Frickley to say that George had been stabbed and Joe had run off in pursuit of the attacker. By the time the two women, accompanied by Alec and Julia Staines, and Les Tanner and Sylvia Goodson, got to the bar, the police and paramedics were in attendance.

Because of his general beefiness, George was not seriously injured. He had lost some blood, but not a great deal, thanks to the intervention of a first-aider from the pub's staff, and he needed only four stiches and a tetanus injection, both administered by the paramedics in the back of their ambulance. He would be fine in a few days and needed to see his GP when he returned to England, to have the stitches removed.

Inspector Gallego had arrived to take charge of the matter from the police end, and his men were in the process of taking statements from George, Owen and other witnesses when the 3rd Age Club party arrived.

Sheila and Brenda gave him both barrels, but he remained unrepentant. "I did all I was obliged to do, I did all I could do. And now your Señor Murray has done the foolish thing and gone in pursuit of this woman."

"And Joe might catch her," Alec Staines said, "but he couldn't punch his way out of a burst balloon. She'll make mincemeat of him."

Accurate it might have been, but it was not the wisest

thing he could have said, and it merely prompted another round of accusation, recrimination and rebuttal between the two women and Gallego.

It was turned eleven when they got back to the hotel, from where Brenda rang Gemma.

"A little late, isn't it?" Sheila asked while her best friend waited for an answer.

"It's only ten o'clock in England."

Brenda was proved right when Gemma answered, and the news was delivered. After the telephone call, as she shut down her phone, Brenda reported, "Gemma is hauling this Higginshaw bloke in tomorrow. She'll go to town on him."

"I'll try Joe again."

Both had tried to ring him several times from outside *The Cock & Bull*, but there had been no answer. Sheila tried again and got no reply.

And they continued to try at intervals throughout the night, but the result was the same.

Ten o'clock in the morning saw the unusually morose group of Sanford 3rd-agers meet on the upper bar terrace, away from the swimming pools and general clutter of the sun loungers and pool bar.

In answer to questions, George reported that he was sore but otherwise in rude health, and Sheila had nothing to tell them other than detail their fruitless efforts to contact Joe, and that Inspector Gallego was due to arrive anytime.

"In summary then," Les Tanner said, "as matters stand, we have no idea whether Murray is dead or alive?"

"We should try to be optimistic, Les," Brenda said. "We know that Joe had his passport and money with him. We're hoping the reason he isn't answering is because he's run for the airport and a flight home."

Sylvia Goodson deployed a pale, pink parasol over her shoulder as a shelter against the fierce sun. "Excuse me, Sheila, Brenda, but surely if Joe was carrying his passport then that must have been his intention all the time."

"Sadly not, Sylvia," Sheila replied and explained Joe's lack of trust in hotel room safes. "Whenever he went out, he always kept his passport and money buried in a deep pocket in his gilet."

"Or in his money belt," Brenda said.

Gallego arrived a few minutes later, but there was little that he could add.

"We have an all points warning on this Ms Killington, and on your friend, Señor Murray, but I do not hope for a result."

His announcement met with a gabble of protest, which he moved quickly to quell.

"Please, ladies and gentlemen, you must understand, Majorca is busy. Tourists arrive and depart by the thousand every day of the week, and there are many ways of coming to and leaving the island. Airlines, ferries, even men with boats who will spirit them away to Ibiza or Menorca or further away for enough money. It would be perfectly possible for Killington and even your friend Murray to slip away unnoticed. We are in the process of issuing a European Arrest Warrant for Ms Killington, but it could be many months or perhaps years before she shows up, and even then, for the warrant to be effective, she must be in a European country. I am sorry for your loss. I am sorry for your pain. But there is no more I can do."

In the dull silence which followed his final words, Tanner struck up the very thought no one else would entertain. "Let us look on the black side, Inspector. If something has happened to Murray, surely we would get to know sooner rather than later?"

Gallego shrugged. "There are many ways of arriving and leaving, Señor, and there are just as many ways of disposing of a body. But I must say, there is nothing to indicate that Joe Murray has come to any harm. And he is a man. He would be able to defend himself against a woman? No?"

Brenda fumed. "Ignoring your blatant sexism, Inspector, I'd say you were wrong. Most of us have known Joe all his life, and he is not a fighter. He never was."

George Robson confirmed it. "Put him up against a ten-year-old girl and he'd be punching above his weight. In a one-to-one with this tart, the smart money would be on her."

Gallego shrugged again. "In that case, I can only say again, there is nothing to tell us that Señor Murray has come to any harm. I will be in touch with your British police, to bring them up to date so that they may search for these two people, but beyond that, there is nothing more I can do. I am sorry."

***

Gemma entered the interview room at Harrogate's main police station a little after ten thirty.

The station commander and the head of the local CID had agreed to let her lead the interview with Higginshaw, accompanied by Detective Constable Lacey, a man of about 30, only recently out of his probationary period.

Having spent twenty minutes on the phone with Sheila Riley, and been brought fully up to date on the situation in Majorca, Gemma was in a bitter mood. Higginshaw, she had vowed, would not walk away from the interview without a charge hanging over him. Attempted fraud was the minimum Gemma would settle for, and she would prefer conspiracy to murder.

With Roger Albiston, the duty solicitor at his side, Higginshaw had the air of a worried man about him, and that suited Gemma. After the introductions were dealt with and recorded, she turned Denise Latham's computer to face him and prepared to run the video.

For the benefit of the tape, she said, "I am about to show Mr Higginshaw a video recording taken by Denise Latham and held on her laptop. The video is dated February sixteenth, ten days before Ms Latham met her death in a road traffic accident."

Gemma hit the keys and sat back while Higginshaw watched the eight-minute recording.

When it had finished, she turned the laptop back to face herself, closed it down and handed it to Detective Constable Lacey for bagging and labelling as evidence.

71

She concentrated on her suspect. "You've seen the video, Mr Higginshaw. Do you have anything to say about it?"

"No. Should I?"

Gemma evaded the question. "You are currently on long-term sick, having suffered a fall on a building site last year. Is that correct?"

"Yes."

"And as a result of that fall, you claim to be all-but totally disabled, in respect of which, you are making a claim for around two million pounds against North Shires Insurance. Is that also correct?"

"Yep. It's no big secret." Higginshaw's casual remark belied his anxiety.

"Would you agree that the video you've just seen casts doubt upon your claim?"

He laughed nervously. "I dunno. Does it?"

"I'm asking the questions, Mr Higginshaw, and I'd be obliged if you'd answer them."

"All right, so I know what it looks like. But I never said I couldn't do nothing at all. I just said I can't follow my regular employment. I'm a builder. A brickie. That's hard graft, that is. Sure I can climb a few steps up a ladder, but I'd never get up one with a full hod on my back. And there's no way I could stand up all day laying bricks. I'm snookered, see. Self-employed with a trick set of bones thanks to that fall, and no one in his right mind is gonna sub work to me. They wouldn't know if the job would ever get done."

Gemma ignored most of the reply. "The day after she took that video, Denise Latham spoke to you, and her report is on this same computer." She delved into the official folder and took out a copy which she passed to the solicitor, and for the benefit of the tape said, "I am furnishing Mr Higginshaw's legal advisor with a copy of Ms Latham's statement." She concentrated once more on her suspect. "In her report Ms Latham indicates that when confronted with the evidence, you became verbally abusive and threatened her with physical violence if she did not leave. Would you agree with that?"

Higginshaw looked to his lawyer who after searching and reading the relevant part of the statement, gave the slightest of nods.

"Yeah, all right, so I mouthed off a bit. It didn't mean nothing. She was a tough little cookie. Dunno that I'd have been able to slap her about a bit. I was angry. Right?"

"And was your wife angry?"

The question threw Higginshaw. "Dawn? She wasn't even there."

"I noticed that too. Throughout all her reports and surveillance, Denise never mentions Mrs Higginshaw once. And yet, less than two weeks later, Denise's car was run off the road and she was killed."

Higginshaw's colour paled. "Well, that wasn't Dawn. She wouldn't do nothing like that."

"Where is she, Tom?"

"I told you the other day, I don't know. She walked out on me months back. Two, three months. At least. I told you."

Gemma switched tack again. Her tone was friendly, offhand. "She have passport, does she? Dawn?"

The question puzzled Higginshaw again. "What? Well, course she does. Everyone has a passport, don't they?"

"Not everyone," Gemma disagreed. "Go on foreign holidays a lot, do you?"

He relaxed a little. "Used to do. Not since the accident mind."

"Ever go to Majorca?"

Again, he shrugged. "A time or two, yeah. Look—"

"Palmanova?"

"What?"

"Did you ever holiday in Palmanova, Majorca?"

"Not that I remember. What is this?"

"I'd be interested to know, too, Inspector," Albiston, the solicitor said. "This line of questioning appears to be leading nowhere."

Gemma persevered. "I'm simply trying to ascertain whether your client or his wife ever visited Majorca, which they have, and whether they were familiar with Palmanova. In fact, I'm trying to learn if Mrs Higginshaw is in Palmanova right now."

"But I don't understand what—"

Higginshaw cut off the solicitor. "I shouldn't think so."

"Then where is she, Mr Higginshaw?"

"I don't know."

"Well, let me tell you what I think." Gemma leaned aggressively forward. "I think you do know, and I think you know that she's in Palmanova... or she was last night, and she's been there for several days, during which time she's made at least three attempts on the life of a Sanford resident, Mr Joe Murray."

"Well—"

"And Joe Murray is the, 'shortarse' you described to me the other day when I called at your house. The shortarse who was following you with Denise Latham."

"Well you're wrong."

Gemma ignored the denial. "You see, Mr Higginshaw, we believe that Denise was murdered. We believe that the accident was not an accident at all, but a deliberate and calculated collision, designed to run her off the road and take her life. That, coupled to the attacks on Mr Murray, lead us to conclude that you and your wife were the only people with sufficient motive to carry out the attack. Two million motives, Mr Higginshaw."

"I said you're wrong."

A question struck Gemma out of the blue and she posed it. "What was your wife's maiden name?"

"I, er... what?"

"I think you heard me, Mr Higginshaw. What was your wife's maiden name?"

There was a brief pause. "Cavanagh. Why?"

This time it was the answer which dropped the spanner in the works, and Gemma was caught out. She hid her surprise. "Did she ever use the name Killington?"

"Nope."

"You're sure?"

"Absolutely."

"Even before you met her?"

Higginshaw modified his answer. "Well, obviously, I mean, I dunno, do I, but I don't see why she should."

Gemma pushed a pad and pen across the table. "Write down her full name and maiden name for me."

Ten minutes later, taking a break as agreed with Albiston, Gemma came out of the room and asked the local team to track down all that was known about the woman.

"You're sure you have this right, ma'am?" Lacey asked.

"It has to be here. There's no one else who fits the profile. This was the only case Denise Latham was working on, and Higginshaw already admitted to me that he'd recognised Joe and Denise. And before you ask, it wouldn't take long for them to learn Joe's name. He's famous all over Sanford."

***

Thirty minutes later they resumed. Still waiting for the information on Dawn, Gemma pressed ahead and as the morning dragged on, Higginshaw became more and more anxious, especially when questioned about his wife.

"I keep telling you I don't know where she is. Why do you keep asking? I don't know."

"Inspector," Albiston put in, "Mr Higginshaw has repeatedly answered the question and denied any knowledge of his wife's whereabouts. Now, I must insist you move the interview on or let him go."

"He's going nowhere, Mr Albiston. May I remind you that this is a murder investigation—"

"Dawn did not kill that woman," Higginshaw interrupted.

Still talking to the solicitor, Gemma insisted, "And that is why I keep going over the same ground." She switched her focus to the suspect. "How do you know she didn't,

Tom?"

"She… she wouldn't."

"You don't know that because you don't know where she is."

"I'm telling you, I know it wasn't her. It can't be."

"She's in Majorca, isn't she?"

"No."

"How do you know? You don't know where she is."

"It's not Dawn."

Higginshaw's insistence led Gemma to conclude that she was onto something. She softened her approach. "Mr Higginshaw… Tom, we understand, believe me. Denise and Joe, well they stuffed you, didn't they? Caught you out and cost you two million quid. Hell, I'd be annoyed with them, too. You want revenge. Or maybe not. Maybe you wanted to stop the report getting to North Shires. It's understandable. Just tell me what you worked out and how. How did you know that Denise hadn't sent the report in yet? Did she tell you that? Or do you have a contact at the North Shires office?"

"I didn't… we didn't… no… I mean… it's not her. Not Dawn. She couldn't, I mean she wouldn't."

"Fine. I accept that. Maybe you were not involved. Maybe Dawn decided to do this off her own bat. But help me prove it, Tom. Tell me where I can find her. Because I will find her. I have a team looking for her right now, and sooner or later, we'll find her, and when we do, she will tell us everything. She'll tell us because I have witnesses who can identify her."

"It's not her."

"If you're so sure, it means you know where she is."

Tears sparked in his eyes. Gemma recognised the symptoms. He was on the verge of cracking, but too hard a push now might send him over the edge.

"Just tell me, Tom. Save yourself all this pain and tell me where I can find her."

He broke down weeping, head resting on his forearms. And when he looked up, his face was lined with agony.

Gemma felt a twinge of sympathy for him. Left alone by a woman who cared nothing for him, yet trying his utmost to remain loyal to her.

She steeled herself. "Where is she, Tom?"

He sobbed and his answer sent shockwaves through Gemma, Lacey and the solicitor.

"In the outhouse. Under the flagstones. Where I buried her."

Chapter Nine

Mick Chadwick, landlord of the Miner's Arms, where the 3rd Age Club held their weekly disco and infrequent, formal meetings, had decked the room with floral tributes, and amongst them he had placed photographs of Joe, sometimes alone, sometimes with other members of the club.

"Not wishing him dead, Sheila," he said, "But you know…"

Sheila nodded her gratitude. Thank you, Michael. I'm not sure Joe would have appreciated it, but we do."

"He wouldn't," Brenda agreed. "He preferred plastic flowers. They were easier to keep clean."

A month had passed since their return from Majorca, and they had heard nothing. In the absence of any concrete evidence, the police, both British and Spanish, refused to declare Joe dead, but neither could they say he was still alive. He had simply disappeared without trace.

So, too, had Ms Killington. She had never been properly identified and if she had come (back) to Great Britain, it was quietly and unobtrusively. Although she was officially still the subject of an all ports warning, and there was a European Arrest warrant sworn out for her, she had never been seen.

Gemma had been commended for her work with Higginshaw. In the days following her abrasive interview, the North Yorkshire police had visited his farmhouse and dug up the flags in outhouse and as promised, they had found Dawn Higginshaw's body, her skull caved in where he had struck her. After a full confession, the builder was on remand awaiting trial for her murder.

And it was to Gemma that the two women, with the

agreement of Les Tanner, the club's new Chair, had turned for the evening.

It was a special meeting, arranged as a tribute to Joe, and Gemma, still many years too young to be allowed membership, had agreed to say a few words in advance of the disco.

The scheduled start time was, as always, eight o'clock. Sheila and Brenda had arrived at seven, and were dressed more formally than usual. It did not surprise either of them as others began to turn out and they too were in more sombre, smarter attire than was customary for the disco. Even George Robson, who had enjoyed his fifteen minutes of fame with a couple of articles in the *Sanford Gazette* on the manner in which had saved Joe's life, was dressed in his best suit.

"It's the one I use for wedding and funerals," he quipped when Brenda mentioned it.

As Chair, Les Tanner, resplendent in a navy blue blazer complete with regimental badge and matching tie called everyone to order at eight, and invited Sheila and Brenda to take the small dais by the windows.

"We promise not to waffle," Sheila said. "We all know why we're here tonight. We're missing a dear friend."

"And employer," Brenda added.

Sheila smiled wanly. "Of all us, we feel we knew Joe the best. Brenda?"

"That's right. But we want to call on someone who knew him even better than us. His niece, Detective Inspector Gemma Craddock."

The two women led the applause and as Gemma moved to the front of the room, silence fell.

She placed a glass of vodka and her notes on the table before her, tucking them in between the disco turntables. "You'll forgive me, ladies and gentlemen. I'm not used to making speeches, but Mrs Riley and Mrs Jump asked, and as Joe's niece I felt it only right that I should pay tribute to him."

She looked out across the assembled faces; sad,

respectful, expectant.

"We all know Joe. And despite what Mrs Jump said, you probably know him better than me. You should do. You've known him longer than me. Short in stature, even shorter in temper, never better than grumpy, outspoken, often to the point of rudeness, he had that awful, Yorkshire tendency to call a spade a bloody shovel and be done with it."

The reminder brought a ripple of chuckles from her audience.

"For the last forty years, he ran his café on Doncaster Road with – we're led to believe – an iron hand and a loud voice. He insulted staff and customers alike. And yet they were faithful to him. The drivers and the shoppers who made their way from the retail park just to sample Joe's inhospitable charms and his excellent food, would never dream of eating elsewhere. And don't forget his crew—" she gestured at Sheila and Brenda, "—who tolerated him until he went too far, and then had the temerity to bring him up short. Not that it worked for long. Joe was like that. You couldn't keep him down."

She let them bask in the memories for a moment.

"But there were other sides to Joe; sides which we never saw enough of. Beneath that gruff exterior beat a heart of solid, twenty-four-carat gold. No matter how much you annoyed him, he would never see you stuck. He would cross the road to help you, if he had to. He donated generously to charities involved with the very young, the elderly, the homeless. And even though he always insisted he had been dragooned into the 3rd Age Club by Mrs Riley and Mrs Jump, he nevertheless worked tirelessly on its behalf… your behalf."

Once more, Gemma paused to let the audience remind itself of this other Joe.

"As a serving detective, I can tell you that Joe is renowned for his low opinion of the police in general. The truth is a long way from that. He had a great deal of respect for the law and the police, but he got irritated when he could see things we could not. He was, you see, a great believer in justice. He loathed crime and criminals. When he set out to crack a crime, no matter how small or large, it was with a determination to see that the culprits never got away with it. He made it his business to see the felons answered for their actions. And that is the Joe I remember. The dogged, determined observer of people and their habits, and the little things that would give them away."

This time Gemma paused to ensure her own emotions were in check.

"It seems odd that when his life was under threat he managed to bring yet another murderer to justice. I would swear it was quite inadvertent, but I suspect that if Joe were here, he'd claim it was intentional. Whichever way you look at it, if he had not put us onto Denise Latham's computer, we would not have uncovered the murder of Dawn Higginshaw and brought her husband to answer for it quite so quickly."

Gemma picked up her glass.

"It's sad that we don't know what happened to Joe. We don't know if he's alive or dead, whether he's in heaven, in hell or in hiding, but I believe in optimism. I like to think he's still out there somewhere, waiting for the chance to come home, and if so, I just hope that he's found the contentment which always seemed to evade him here in Sanford." She raised her glass. "Ladies and gentlemen, I give you Joe Murray."

As one, the audience raised their glasses and called out, "Joe."

THE END

Fantastic Books
Great Authors

CROOKED
CAT

Meet our authors and discover
our exciting range:

- Gripping Thrillers
- Cosy Mysteries
- Romantic Chick-Lit
- Fascinating Historicals
- Exciting Fantasy
- Young Adult and Children's
  Adventures

Visit us at:
www.crookedcatbooks.com

Join us on facebook:
www.facebook.com/crookedcatbooks

16459849R00051

Printed in Great Britain
by Amazon